OXYGEN DEPRIVED

BY

BOOK 3 IN THE KILGORE FIRE SERIES
LANI LYNN VALE

Lani Lynn Vale

Copyright © 2016 Lani Lynn Vale

All rights reserved.

**ISBN-13:
978-1535319058**

**ISBN-10:
1535319054**

Dedication

To my lovely children who have done nothing but scream, cry, complain and fight. I love you without conditions. Without you, I would have never started writing. I love you more than you'll ever know.

Acknowledgements

FuriousFotog: Thank you so much for taking these photos for me. They're beautiful, and you have such incredible talent it's unreal.

Gary Taylor- One day I'll meet you! And when that day comes- I'll tell you in person just like I'm writing you now, that you are a very beautiful person inside and out. Thank you so much for posing for this photo. You make a wonderful Drew!

CONTENTS

Prologue- Page 9
Chapter 1- Page 15
Chapter 2- Page 25
Chapter 3- Page 31
Chapter 4- Page 41
Chapter 5- Page 51
Chapter 6- Page 59
Chapter 7- Page 69
Chapter 8- Page 77
Chapter 9- Page 105
Chapter 10- Page 115
Chapter 11- Page 139
Chapter 12- Page 145
Chapter 13- Page 165
Chapter 14- Page 179
Chapter 15- Page 191
Chapter 16- Page 201
Chapter 17- Page 213
Chapter 18- Page 219
Chapter 19- Page 233
Chapter 20- Page 241
Chapter 21- Page 255
Chapter 22- Page 267
Epilogue- Page 277

Other Titles by Lani Lynn Vale:

The Freebirds

Boomtown

Highway Don't Care

Another One Bites the Dust

Last Day of My Life

Texas Tornado

I Don't Dance

The Heroes of The Dixie Wardens MC

Lights To My Siren

Halligan To My Axe

Kevlar To My Vest

Keys To My Cuffs

Life To My Flight

Charge To My Line

Code 11- KPD SWAT Series

Center Mass

Double Tap

Bang Switch

Execution Style

Charlie Foxtrot

Kill Shot

Coup De Grace

The Uncertain Saints MC

Whiskey Neat

Jack & Coke

Vodka On The Rocks

Bad Apple

Dirty Mother

Rusty Nail

Kilgore Fire

Shock Advised

Flash Point

Oxygen Deprived

Controlled Burn

Lani Lynn Vale

PROLOGUE

They said eat your vegetables. I said eat shit and die.
-Aspen's younger thoughts

Aspen

Twenty years earlier
Beavers Bend. Broken Bow, Oklahoma

I watched him play football for nearly an hour with my brother, completely and totally enraptured by him.

"Mom!" I hissed at my mother. "Do you see that teenage boy over there?"

My mother turned from the magazine that was in her hands, to me.

"Yes, baby," she said. "What about him?"

Everyone had seen him. I'm not sure why I was bothering pointing the man—*teenager*—out to her.

"I'm going to marry him," I informed her.

She blinked.

"What?" She whispered in shock. "Why do you say that?"

I looked back over at the teenager, that wasn't so much of a teenager but more of a young man on his way to adulthood, and back to her.

"We just are. I've decided."

She laughed.

"You've decided, huh?" She teased.

I nodded.

"And how are you going to accomplish that?" She wondered.

"She's going to demand it of him, Mother," Downy, my brother who wasn't very happy about being on vacation with us, drawled.

Downy and the teenager were probably similar in age, although that's where the similarities ended.

Downy had red hair, where the teenager had blonde.

Downy's ugly eyes had nothing on the teenager's gray eyes that looked like they were ringed with green.

I couldn't tell for certain, though, which was why I moved closer.

And found myself next to a couple that was excited about something.

"He's getting married," the woman was saying to the man. "To Constance. Isn't that something?"

The man shrugged. "She's not the best, but I guess she could be worse."

The woman snorted. "Don't let him hear you say that. They've been dating for four years now. And he knows everything, don't you know?"

The man sighed.

"She's cried every night this week because he's been gone to the fire academy. How do you think she's going to fare when he's gone once every three days?" The man continued.

The woman had nothing to say to that, and I sat down in the chair right by them, hoping it wasn't obvious what I was doing. I crossed my legs and started swinging my foot.

Then in a rush of moving limbs, the teenager took the seat, in between his parents and me.

He had his shirt off, and his skin was bronzed from the summer sun.

"Your mother tells me you're getting married," the man said to his son.

"Yep," he confirmed.

"Why?"

The teenager paused. "Because I love her, Dad."

My heart thumped painfully, and I couldn't help but look over at the three of them.

I must have made a small noise because the father's eyes went to me, then back to his son.

"But why do you love her?" He asked.

The teenager paused.

"Because, I just do."

"You should really have a better answer than that," I blurted out, immediately clamping my hands over my mouth.

All three of them looked over to me.

"What?" The teenager asked shortly.

I dropped my hands and smiled weakly, suddenly feeling incredibly stupid for offering my two cents when it wasn't asked for.

My mother was always getting on to me about that, too.

"Uhh," I said.

"Go on, child. Tell him what you meant," the father urged.

I bit my lip.

"It's just...if you really love her, you should know why you love her. You should be able to say more than 'because I just do.' You should love her because she makes you feel happy. Because she makes you sleep well at night. Because she makes you laugh. Because when you see her, your heart starts to race. Things like that," I informed him. "*'I just do'* isn't a good enough reason. "

He blinked, surprised at how well I'd answered him.

And the father smiled.

"What she said."

"Well," the teenager growled. "You can't take a ten-year-old's opinion for shit, Dad. They don't know anything."

My mouth dropped open in affront.

"That wasn't called for," I blurted.

My brother showed up at my side, pulling me away from the three of them.

"She's sorry," Downy apologized to them. "She doesn't realize how nosy she really is."

I snatched my hand away from my brother.

"Get off me, you infidel," I ordered crossly.

Downy laughed in my face, then dropped me back off to my mother before returning to the field.

It didn't take long for the teenager to join Downy, and soon they had a full on football game again with a couple of other kids.

And I watched, and wondered, if maybe I was wrong about the teenager.

Maybe my instincts were off.

Then I decided that no, my instincts weren't off. *His* probably were, though

He would be mine.

It might take a while, but he would.

No ifs, ands or buts about it.

Lani Lynn Vale

CHAPTER 1

Men and women are different. If a man is scorned, he'll show up at night. If a woman is scorned, she'll show up at your job and smash your shit in front of everyone.
-Proven Fact

Aspen

I stood at my front window, eyes narrowed as I watched man after man move heavy boxes out of the back of a moving truck into the house directly across the street from mine.

Every single one of the men that were helping were all drop dead gorgeous...and I knew them *all*.

It was kind of hard not to when the fire station was right next door to the police station.

If I didn't know them directly, I knew their faces—and that wasn't a good thing, either.

They would know all about my shame.

Would know that...

"I can't believe you're under house arrest," my best friend muttered.

I grimaced at her.

"At least my job lets me work from home," I mumbled darkly.

Somehow, in the light of day, this wasn't anywhere near as *okay* as I thought it'd be.

In fact, once I ran out of milk around two in the afternoon, nothing was funny. Not at all.

"This *suuuucks*!" I whined loudly. "Why did this happen to me?"

There was silence for a few long moments, then my best friend's laughter.

"Probably because you were caught beating the crap out of your ex boyfriend's truck and then his woman," Naomi giggled, laughter filling her voice.

I turned my glare on her.

"Shut your face," I growled through clenched teeth. "Or I swear, by all that's holy, I'll shove that coke can up your ass."

Naomi could no longer contain her laughter, and she fell to the floor with the hilarity of it all.

Me, on the other hand, yeah, I didn't find it nearly as funny as she did.

Naomi continued to laugh until tears rolled down her cheeks, but I stared at her for long moments, letting my dissatisfaction show.

"I'm sorry," she gasped, trying to catch her breath. "But you'd laugh at me, too, if our roles were reversed."

I sighed.

She was right, I would.

I wouldn't be able to help myself.

However, I was the one in this situation, not her, so it was hard to say what I would and wouldn't do under different circumstances.

I crossed my feet out in front of me and stared at the blank wall where my TV used to be.

Danny had taken it while I was in jail, along with my Xbox, the controllers, my Dish satellite receiver and all of my kitchen appliances that were small enough to fit into his mom's SUV.

How did I know this?

Because my neighbors told me.

They'd spent hours telling me how they watched him take everything.

"Why does your cat have a note attached to her neck?" Naomi asked, her eyes caught by the sight of the white paper that stood out starkly against my cat's black fur.

"He's a whore," I said simply.

"Why?" she asked, crawling on her hands and knees toward the cat.

She stopped, read the note, and then snorted out a laugh.

"She's a muffin stealing whore?" Naomi asked.

I nodded.

"I was bored," I said. "I even took his picture and submitted it to Ellen for that pet shaming contest she's got going on."

"Ellen? *The Ellen DeGeneres Show*?" Naomi asked. "I don't think Ellen does that."

"Well, she should," I muttered. "Speaking of Ellen, she's on!"

I was now on day two of my five-month house arrest, and I was fairly sure by day seven, it was very likely I'd be bouncing off the walls.

Naomi and I watched about five minutes of it before she stood, stretching her arms up high over her head.

"I'm going to Wal-Mart. Do you want me to get you anything?" She wondered. "I'll drop it off tomorrow on the way to pick the kids up from school."

I shot up off the couch and ran to my office, picking up a piece of white computer paper and folding it in half.

Once I was sure the marker wouldn't bleed through, I picked up the only writing utensil I could ever seem to find, a Sharpie, and quickly wrote down a list.

Once I had that done, I walked back to the kitchen where I pulled out seven twenties and walked back towards where Naomi was still standing, watching the show in front of her.

"Here," I said. "This is my list."

"Aspen," Naomi started. "This only has a TV on it."

I nodded.

"Yep," I agreed.

"But, I thought the chief of police ordered Danny to give all your stuff back," Naomi sounded confused. "That doesn't make sense to get you a TV."

I gave her a look. "Does your brother ever do what he's supposed to do?" I asked. "I doubt he ever follows orders unless The Chief makes him do it, and even then he'd actually have to come over to ask me whether he gave it back. It's not like Danny's going to offer up that information."

Naomi grimaced.

"My brother's a dumbass," she muttered under her breath. "I'll get your TV back for you, but I'm not spending this money on it. I'll buy you groceries instead."

"Hmm," I said. "Just make sure you get me some cheese squares."

"Aspen," Naomi hesitated. "You can't eat like that when you have no way to workout. You're gonna get fat."

"I've got it all planned out," I evaded. "I can go all the way to the end of my yard on the back side, and all the way to the sidewalk in the front. It's exactly five thousand two hundred and eighty feet if I make the loop around seven and a half times."

She looked at me.

"How'd you figure that out?" She tilted her head.

I shrugged.

"I got bored this afternoon, and my uncle left that roll thing that measures out distance," I pointed to the measuring tape that was on the table next to the door.

She snorted.

"Okay," she said. "I'll bring you some food back tomorrow. And if my brother doesn't drop the TV off, I'll make sure to bring you one."

I threw my hands around my best friend.

"You know I don't blame you, right?" I confirmed.

She sighed.

"Yes," she nodded. "But I'm the one who set you up with him in the first place. I thought he'd changed his ways. Had I known he was just going to go back to his cheating and whoring around, I would've never given him the permission to date you."

I gave her a look.

"Since when has my boyfr—err…your brother done anything that he was supposed to do?" I raised a brow. "You could've told him all day long to stay away from me, but he would've inevitably done exactly what he wanted to do in the end."

"Well," she headed to the door. "It doesn't mean I have to be happy about it."

I stared at the back of her head. "Naomi," I muttered. "Don't do anything stupid."

"Stupid?" She said sweetly. "Never."

***

A banging at my door woke me up.

I startled, sitting up and dislodging the cat from my feet, effectively pissing him off and justifying the attack he launched on my feet not two seconds later.

"Motherfucking cock-sucker!" I growled, yanking my feet away.

The cat looked up at me with his adorable, mutinous eyes.

"Go fuck yourself, Urchin," I growled.

Urchin didn't bother to look innocent anymore, instead he hissed at me.

"Fucker," I muttered as I hauled my annoyed and sleepy butt out of bed.

Grabbing a robe, which just so happened to belong to Danny, and wrapping it around my shoulders, I walked to the front door and peeked through the peephole.

My eyes narrowed and my lip curled in disdain as I took in my ex-boyfriend, the bane of my existence, on the other side of the door.

"What do you want?" I asked him, looking back over my shoulder at the clock above my fire place.

Three in the morning. Awesome.

"My sister's making me bring the TV back. If you want it inside, I suggest you open the door or I'll leave it on the front porch. And we both know you won't be able to move it," Danny said nastily.

"Just leave it," I ordered. "I'll get Jonah or Downy to move it tomorrow."

Danny had the nerve to laugh.

"Go away," I growled through the door.

He did, making sure to take the TV to the very border of my yard first.

Danny left, but not before he accidentally knocked the TV over, leaving it sprawling in the wet grass just outside of my ankle bracelet's range.

"Son of a bitch," I growled, yanking open the door in time to see Danny speed off in that stupid – but nice – pickup truck of his that we'd picked out together. Although I did manage a small smile when I noticed it still looked a bit worse for the wear.

I walked down the sidewalk, stopping just at the edge of my yard.

I stared down at the ankle bracelet, lifting my robe out of the way, and tested it.

The instant my foot went out of range, it started blinking red.

Then Mrs. Fairchild's words drifted through my brain.

"You'll have ten seconds to get back in the safe zone, or a police cruiser will be sent to your house to see why you've stepped out of your yard."

Grimacing, I moved back inside my yard and stared at the TV.

It was definitely deliberate.

"Damn him!" I growled in pure frustration.

The sound of a door opening from across the street had me looking up in time to see my new neighbor come out with a pretty lady latched onto him.

He gave her one hell of a hot, wet kiss and then lifted his head from the woman's mouth.

"'G'night," the man muttered, setting the woman away from him. "Thanks for helping."

My brows rose.

Was that code for *'thanks for sucking my cock?'*

The man's eyes came to me when the woman went to her car, giggling and waving over her shoulder the entire way.

He watched me, but I turned my eyes down to the TV once again.

The car finally left, and I sighed, turning around and heading back to my front door.

"You getting rid of that?" I heard, the man's voice a lot closer to me than he'd been when I started heading back to my door.

I turned to find him standing in the middle of the street.

"No, I just got it back. Last time I checked, it worked fine," I replied. "But I can't get it back in my house."

"Why's it outside in the first place?" He wanted to know.

I pinched my lips as I glared at the man.

"Because my ex-boyfriend dropped it off there, knowing damn well I couldn't get it."

"Interesting," he said. "Do you want me to bring it in?"

I weighed the benefits of getting the TV inside against the possibility that he might be a serial killer.

Knowing damn well I couldn't live without the TV, I decided to take a chance with my life and said, "Please."

The man didn't even hesitate. I quickly moved out of his way, sweeping my hand through the night air in an embellished fashion to direct him towards my door.

"After you," I murmured.

He picked the TV up as if it weighed nothing, and easily walked up the path and into the house, stopping once he was in the living room.

"Where do you want it?" He stopped.

I pursed my lips and pointed to where it used to be.

"It used to be right there, hanging above the mantle, but if the wall mount wasn't laying out there with the TV, then you'll have to just put it on the floor, I guess," I pointed to a blank spot where the recliner I'd bought Danny used to sit.

His brows furrowed at my mention of him taking the mount, but he placed it on the floor anyway, stepping back once I had.

"Thank you," I sighed softly. "I really appreciate it."

Now get out of my house, please. I don't really want to die.

He must've sensed my thoughts because he headed to the door without another word, not stopping until he was down at the end of my yard standing next to my mailbox.

"Don't let him into your house anymore," he said. "And I'd suggest changing your locks. If you want to get new locks, I'll put them on for you."

I lifted my robe up slightly to show my anklet monitor.

"No can do, sir. I can't go out even if I wanted to," I informed him.

His eyes went down to my ankle, his gaze being captured by the blinking red dot.

"You're on house arrest?" He wondered, surprise evident in his voice.

I nodded. "Yep."

"Why?" He pushed.

There was no way he didn't know.

None.

I'd been the talk of the county; my own brother was a cop.

There was seriously no way he didn't know why I was on house arrest, but I decided to tell him anyway.

Tomorrow.

Instead of saying goodbye, or even a 'see you tomorrow' I closed the door without another word.

I couldn't handle anymore adulting right now.

Tomorrow would be soon enough.

CHAPTER 2

I'd rather ask for forgiveness than permission.
-Rule of thumb

Aspen

"No, no, no," I cried, watching as the smoke started to pour out of the open oven door. "Why? *Whyyyy?*" My questioning exclamation came out in a pitifully whiny and frustrated twang that I just couldn't help.

Today was New Year's Eve, seven days after my asshole ex got me put on house arrest, and I was going stir crazy.

I'd cleaned everything, top to bottom, and the house was immaculate now. There wasn't one thing I would need to clean for at least a month.

However, now I needed to focus on getting the smoke out, or I might suffocate to death in my own house.

Walking to the window above the kitchen sink, I pushed it out and open.

The smoke billowed out, and I was amazed at just how much smoke one little turkey could produce.

"Surely, it can't be that bad," I murmured to myself, coughing slightly when I pushed further into the kitchen to come to a stop in front of the stove.

I grabbed the oven mitts beside the oven, thrust my hands into them, and then bent over to grab the turkey from the oven.

It was heavy.

Really heavy.

But I managed to finagle it out and onto the kitchen counter without too much fuss.

It was then I got my first good look at the turkey.

"Black's probably not okay to eat," a man said from behind me.

I gasped, turning around to see a man in full turn out fire gear behind me and right behind him were two more.

The one closest to me, though, was my newest neighbor. The one I couldn't stop thinking about.

The one who was currently staring at my ass.

"What are you doing in here?" I asked warily, backing my ass up against the counter so he could no longer see my cheeks.

The dastardly man smiled.

Fucking smiled!

"You have smoke coming out of your house," he said as if he was talking to a child. "Smoke, where we come from, means fire. Fire means the fire department comes. Right?"

I glared at him.

"Nothing's on fire," I muttered darkly.

"Well, we didn't know that, and your door was hanging wide open, so…" he shrugged.

I narrowed my eyes at him.

"So you just decided to come in without my explicit permission?" I asked, crossing my arms over my chest and glaring at the man.

"Jesus Christ. Ridley, where the fuck are you?" Downy, my brother, yelled from somewhere beyond the kitchen.

"I'm in the kitchen," I called loudly. "And stop calling me Ridley! My name is fucking Aspen! Use it!"

I hated being called Ridley. By him, most of all.

My name was Aspen Ridley Crew, and ever since I could remember, he'd called me Ridley. I don't know why, and I could never get him to tell me. Yet, it was incredibly annoying. No one called me Ridley. I didn't even like the name Ridley.

"What the fuck are you doing in your underwear?" Downy snapped the moment he saw me.

"Well," I gestured to the room and people around me. "I was by myself up until about thirty seconds ago, so I don't know why I wouldn't be in my underwear if I was in my own goddamned house!"

Downy frowned. "Why are you so mad at me?"

I narrowed my eyes.

"Gee, I don't know," I drawled. "How about you don't ever stop by? Or how about the fact that you only come by when you need something, or I'm potentially burning to death?"

His eyes narrowed.

"And you're half the reason I'm stuck in this hell hole in the first place," I muttered darkly, pushing in between him and my new neighbor. "Go home."

Downy followed me.

"Your ass is hanging out of those," he muttered. "And why can't you ever do anything right?" he asked. "I tried really hard to only get you house arrest. Do you know what could have happened for assaulting a police officer?" He continued. "You could've gone to jail. Not to mention the man's my friend. How does it look to have your sister beat the shit out of your friend?"

I turned around and stared at him incredulously.

"You got the fact that Danny cheated on me, right?" I asked.

He frowned.

"He was with a female officer, and they weren't fucking. They were working," he countered.

I laughed then.

"Yeah," I said. "That female officer was fucking my fiancé. On duty. What would you have done if you'd walked up on Memphis fucking Nico?"

He crossed his arms over his chest. "First of all, Nico has a wife. Second of all, don't bring my wife into this. She would never cheat on me. She's too good of a woman to do so. You must've done something…"

"Don't you dare finish that sentence," I slammed the bedroom door in his face.

I immediately ran to the bed and buried my face into the pillows.

Nobody believed me.

It was the same thing, over and over again, and it was beginning to really get to me.

It hadn't been my fault that he'd cheated. I'd done everything right.

I'd been a fucking awesome girlfriend.

I'd taken his uniforms to and from the dry cleaners.

I'd visited him at work.

I'd brought him dinner to work, which had been what I was doing the night I found him with his hands down the back of his partner's pants and his mouth latched onto her breast.

My first thought had been 'had he forgotten he'd asked me to bring him dinner?'

Then it'd quickly changed into anger. Pure, white hot rage.

I'd been so mad, I couldn't even see straight.

I'd walked back to his truck, which I'd borrowed because I'd taken it to get the oil changed while he was at work.

Then I'd purposefully driven his truck off the road, slamming it into the nearest brick wall I could find, which happened to be the sign that sat in front of the police station.

Before it'd read 'Kilgore Police Department.' Now it just read 'gore.'

Once I'd shaken myself from my stupor of being in a wreck, I'd gotten out of the car and reached for the tire iron that Danny kept in the back for emergency purposes. Then proceeded to take the tire iron to the rest of Danny's truck that hadn't been damaged in the accident.

By the time I'd rounded the truck to the other side and finished off with breaking the glass of the passenger side window, I'd caught the attention of most of the police department.

They'd all stared at me in shock, including my brother.

Then Danny had showed up and completely lost his shit.

So I'd done the only thing I could think of doing, which had been to throw the tire iron at him to keep him from beating the crap out of me.

It'd beamed him right on the forehead, and he'd gone down like a sack of potatoes in front of about ten cops and even more bystanders.

His partner, the bitch who I'd cooked dinner for and let borrow my best dress to go out on a date with a man whose name she refused to tell me.

"God," I moaned. "My life sucks."

Downy had done the best that he could under the circumstances.

Danny was well liked throughout the department, and I'd gone and beaten the crap out of his truck.

I'd brought it all upon myself, and I didn't have anyone to complain to.

Even Naomi, his sister, had been a little appalled at my behavior, and she'd done some pretty sketchy stuff in her time.

"He's gone!" My neighbor yelled through my closed door. "The turkey's out in the trashcan behind your house, and I'm going to lock the door, okay?"

"Thank you," I yelled back, then promptly burst into tears.

CHAPTER 3

14,000 people are having sex right now. 156,000 are kissing. Then there's you. You're reading this instead of getting some.
-Coffee Cup

Drew

I was walking my trashcan out to the trash the next night when the little imp next door came out into her yard, and started wiggling her bare toes in the grass.

"Evening," I said to her almost out of habit.

She snapped her head up.

"Uhh, hi," she smiled slightly.

Jesus, that just did it for me.

I was forty-two years old, and never once in my life had I had a woman affect me like this woman did.

A woman that'd somehow gotten on house arrest and was probably her own special brand of crazy.

"Can you get your trash all the way out?" I asked her.

She nodded, pointing to the trashcan that was barely at the side of the road. Mostly, it was behind her shrubs that lined her mailbox, and I could just see the garbage man missing it.

So, like a nice guy, I walked over and pulled the trashcan down until it sat where it belonged.

"Thanks," she smiled. "I debated whether to even put it out."

I looked down in the trashcan and saw the whole thing filled to the brim with pictures and…clothes?

"You don't need these clothes anymore?" I asked her.

She shook her head.

"You remember that ex-boyfriend I was talking about?" She turned her head.

I nodded, looking up at her and studying her face.

How anyone could leave her was beyond me. She was a freakin' vision.

Although she was really short, I would guess no more than five feet two inches or so, she had long, curly brown hair that fell down to her waist. The biggest blue eyes in Texas, and a beautiful mouth that just begged for kissing.

Her breasts were full and round, just perfect. Not too big, not too small.

They'd probably fit perfectly in my mouth…

Shit!

I tore my eyes away from her breasts, turning them to gaze at the shrub behind her house, and immediately winced.

"You need to get that tree/shrub thing trimmed," I said off handedly.

I wasn't able to turn off the firefighter in me. It was always there in the background, pulsing like a living thing deep inside me.

She turned to study the tree where it was brushing the power line above it and shrugged indifferently.

"I don't have the money to pay for that right now," she admitted. "It's taking almost my whole month's paycheck just to cover my rent, my car—which, might I add, I'm not allowed to use—and the costs to pay for my house arrest."

I could tell that she really didn't want to admit that.

"Get your brother to take care of it," I told her.

She shook her head.

"If I had my way, I wouldn't ever have to talk to him again," she admitted. "Thanks for putting my trash out. If you have a chance after they empty it, could you push it back into my yard?"

I nodded.

"I can," I said, knowing when to shut up.

She smiled sadly at me and then turned to go to the side of her house.

I stayed watching her for way too long and ended up seeing her again about a minute later when she came out on the other side of her house next to the offending shrub I'd told her to trim.

She didn't lift her gaze from the ground as she walked, turned the corner at the front of her yard and then disappeared down the side of the house.

Shaking my head, I pulled the keys to my truck out of my pocket and unlocked the doors.

The locks clicked open and I got inside, enjoying the new car smell that assaulted my senses the moment I got inside.

Pushing the button to the window, I lowered it nearly all the way, shivering slightly at the way the cold hit me to the bone.

As I backed out of the driveway, after starting it, I idly wondered why she didn't have shoes on, but chose not to give it, or her, too much thought.

She was a grown woman.

There was no need for me to be her daddy.

If she wanted to walk around in the nearly twenty-five-degree weather without any shoes on, who was I to say anything?

Of course, thoughts of frostbite on her cute little toes assaulted me all the way to the station. As I pulled in, my mind still hadn't managed to shake off thoughts of her.

I parked in my usual spot, getting out on autopilot as I made my way into the bay where all the firetrucks and ambulances for the city were held.

"How's it going, Naomi?" I asked one of the student paramedics that was obviously working with us today.

She was washing the quint—the fire truck—and I was glad that I didn't have to do that today.

Especially with the wind that blew through not ten seconds later.

"It's going, I guess," she said, a smile always on her face. "Booth was just helping me, but his wife called him about something to do with a pet, so I decided to finish it up for him."

"Thanks," I replied distractedly. "I'm sure he appreciates it."

Naomi grinned.

"Hey," I stopped and turned to look at her. "I saw you at my neighbor's house."

Her brows rose.

"Which one?" She wondered.

"The cute brunette with the ankle monitor," I gestured to my own ankle.

Her brows pinched down in confusion.

"Who?" She asked.

I laughed.

"You know more than one?" I asked laughingly.

She suddenly grinned.

"Well, no," she replied sheepishly. "I only heard half of what you said before I saw him."

She gestured to PD, one of my fellow firefighters.

My eyes followed the big fucker as he tried valiantly to carry about fifteen bags of food from his car at once.

"So?" I asked, turning back to her.

"So what?" She asked distractedly.

Chuckling to myself, I turned and left her to her lustful adoration.

PD was a kinky fucker. If she wasn't into that, he probably wouldn't be into her.

How he got into that shit, I didn't know. But, hey, to each their own, it's not my business to judge what gets him off. I never cited him for his feelings and beliefs.

He could do what he wanted with the women he brought to his bed, and I'd continue to enjoy the ones I brought to my bed my way.

"How's it going," Booth muttered as he stared blankly at the kitchen stove.

"Good," I said. "What's up?"

"Fuckin' dog catcher caught the dog outside our house again," he muttered, sounding miffed.

"Thought you put a new fence in," I mumbled, walking to the fridge and pulling out the eggs and bacon from the top shelf.

"I did," he muttered darkly. "Now I have a hundred and fifty-dollar ticket if I want to get the dog back."

"If?" I drawled.

He grinned then, a rare smile lighting up his face.

"Yep," he agreed. "If."

"Your wife will kick your ass," I told him. "You know that right? Then she'll just go pay the fine anyway and you won't get any sex for a month."

"You know this for certain?" He asked.

I nodded. "Have an ex-wife. We were married for twelve years before we split. Trust me, it's easier in the long run if you just give her what she wants."

"You were married?" Booth asked.

This was the most I'd ever spoken to him with him being the new guy and all, so I decided to keep talking, despite the fact that it still chapped my ass to talk about Constance.

"Yeah," the word a bitter taste in my mouth. "Right out of fire school and everything."

"What happened?" He asked, leaning forward.

I sighed, pulling out the cast iron skillet out of the lower cabinet, then turned on the gas before lighting the burner with the long liter next to the stove.

"She and I grew apart," I said. "She hated me being a firefighter. Hated that I had to work so much to keep us afloat. Her father hated me because I 'made his daughter cry so much.' Which he loved to bring up every possible chance he got. It kept getting worse and worse until she finally filed for divorce."

I dropped a dollop of butter down into the bottom of the pan.

"Do you still love her?" Booth asked.

"No," I admitted. "I guess I felt obligated to stay with her. I would still be there if she hadn't filed, though."

"Kids?" He guessed.

I nodded. "Fifteen-year-old," I nodded. "She turns sixteen this month."

His mouth dropped open.

"You have a sixteen-year-old?" He asked in surprise.

I nodded. "I do."

"Why doesn't she come to any family functions that the department puts on?" He wondered.

I grimaced.

That was a sore subject, and it hurt every time I talked about it.

"She doesn't like that I hurt her mom," I told the truth, but not embellishing any. "And she has free reign to see me anytime she wants. I send child support checks to her mother once a month, but…" I shrugged.

Booth didn't say anything, and I was glad.

At least he knew when a man had enough.

"I want mine over easy," he said mildly.

I nodded.

"Scrambled!" Came Tai's voice from the bathroom.

I snorted out a laugh, then laughed even louder when PD answered from the doorway with Naomi at his back.

"I want mine hard," he said, his eyes drifting to Naomi as he said it.

I made a gagging motion with my finger pointed to my throat, and he winked at me.

He was trying to make her uncomfortable, and by the looks of her scalding red face, he'd accomplished it.

Just before I cracked the first egg, the tone dropped, signaling the first call of the shift.

"Fuck!" Tai called from the bathroom.

I laughed, turning off the gas and making sure the flame was out before I moved everything off the stove and started walking to the garage bay.

"Who's on the medic today?" Naomi asked me as she jogged to catch up.

"Me," I said.

I was usually the driver of the truck, but once every two weeks I worked the medic to keep my skills fresh, today being one of those days.

"Oh, yay," she drawled sarcastically.

I tossed her a look that clearly said, 'shut up.'

She closed her mouth and shut up, going to the side door of the ambulance and getting in the back without another word.

I got in the passenger seat, then pressed the 'en route' button on the screen to help Tai out. When a call came in, we had two minutes to get in the truck and go. By pressing it, I gave Tai a couple more seconds. A, because I wanted to, and B, because I didn't want to have my ass chewed out by the captain because we didn't respond to a call in less than the time we were allotted.

Speaking of which, Tai came running out of the door to the living quarters like his ass was on fire, buttoning his pants and fastening his belt as he did.

"Sorry," he apologized breathlessly as he got in the front seat. "My wife decided to try something new for dinner last night, and it went straight through me. All night long."

I snorted, reaching up to press the garage door button once we'd made it outside fully.

That's when the rain decided to change to sleet.

"Shit," Tai groaned. "This is already getting bad."

I looked at the road, watching as the further we went from the station, the worse it seemed to get.

"Medic three, we have a two vehicle accident on South Main. Two extractions needed. Third vehicle's occupant up and walking around." The dispatcher called through our radios.

"Fucking perfect," Tai sighed. "The busiest freakin' road in Kilgore, and we're working a call on it."

We got there less than five minutes later, and when I stepped foot on the icy white ground, I slipped.

I caught myself on the side of the medic, then shuffled awkwardly to the back of the ambulance.

"Naomi," I called. "When you get out I want you to start doing a perimeter check."

She looked at the cars, then nodded, seeing the empty car seats just like I had.

"Got it," she agreed, stepping out of the back.

I caught her before she could fall on her face, and I said, "Please be careful."

She nodded, smiled, and we started working.

I saw her the entire time out of my peripheral vision while I worked on stabilizing the two patients in the two separate cars.

I saw she'd gone to the third guy, the one who'd been up and walking around, and started questioning him.

I'd just turned around when I heard the screech of tires, followed by the terrified screams of Naomi.

As I whipped my head around, I witnessed every firefighter's worst nightmare.

CHAPTER 4

I wish I could stab idiots with my head.
-Unicorn

Drew

My drive home was almost on autopilot.

I hadn't realized I'd even made it onto my street until the turn into my driveway was suddenly upon me.

I pulled in and nearly laughed when I saw Aspen trying to check her mail.

She was balanced on the mailbox, leaning over and around it as she struggled to reach the paper that was in the very back of the box.

Putting it into park and getting out, I shut the door then walked across the street.

She looked up almost sheepishly, staring at me like I was Superman.

"Need help?" I asked her.

"Now," she glared. "What would give you that idea?"

It was more than obvious that she wasn't in a good mood.

I wasn't either.

"Your friend's going to make it," I told her. "She has a concussion. One of my fellow firefighters pulled her out of the way in time."

Her head dropped and then her shoulders started to shake.

"I feel so terrible," she moaned, pushing away from the mailbox and scooting back three steps before she whirled around and started to hurry to her house.

I got her mail and trashcan, shoved my keys into my pocket and followed after her.

She'd left the door to her house open, so I took that as my indication that I was allowed to come inside.

Dropping the mail onto the front entry table, I closed the door and followed the sounds of sobbing into the kitchen.

Then even further into the master bedroom that was off the kitchen.

I found her face down on her bed.

I wasn't really good at handling crying females.

Hence why I just ignored the problems going on in my marriage instead of tackling them before they got too bad.

"Aspen?" I said softly.

Aspen's tear filled eyes rose, taking me in, and she smiled a watery smile at me.

"I'm hormonal," she whined. "It's the female equivalent of dying, you know?"

No, I didn't know.

Which she got, the longer she looked at me.

"I'm on my period, and I cry a lot for random reasons." She explained more in depth. "And my best friend nearly got run over by a semi-truck today, and I can't even go see her in the hospital because of this stupid piece of crap," she growled in frustration. "Stupid Danny."

"Come sit outside with me," I ordered softly.

I needed to get out of her bedroom.

Even the talk of her being on her period didn't have any effect on my cock.

It was raging, and I was somewhat happy to know it was still functional.

I hadn't gotten a hard on from an actual real live woman in months. Though I'd sure as hell tried multiple times—which ended in embarrassment on my end.

Call me crazy, but I guessed it was related to the fact that a woman had thoroughly fucked me over.

Then my daughter, who I didn't want to admit was a woman yet, had gutted me.

Needless to say, I wasn't very sympathetic to the female plight these days.

"Come outside with me," I ordered, tugging her up into my arms. "It's just raining now and the temperature has warmed up a bit. You can tell me why you're in this mess."

She slowly got up to her hands and knees, then crawled backwards until her feet were both planted firmly on the floor.

"Okay," she mumbled softly.

Thunder boomed overhead.

I looked up at the roof, almost as if just by doing so I would be able to see whatever storm was headed our way.

Instead, I saw a mirror.

A big one.

Needing to get out of there before I had any more crazy thoughts, I grabbed her hand and tugged her along behind me.

"Want a beer?" I asked.

She shook her head as we walked through the rain drops to the side part of the front yard where a little gazebo was sitting.

It was in sore need of a new coat of paint, and would likely need a new swing sometime soon, but I led her there anyway.

"No, thank you," she declined softly. "I'd rather a Dr. Pepper."

I walked away, but continued to talk to her as I did.

"Why are you on house arrest?" I asked, taking a beer from the cooler in the back of my truck.

"I'm officially grounded from alcohol, too. It's one of my stipulations," she admitted.

My brows rose.

"Long story," she muttered.

Lowering the lid of the cooler, I popped the top on the beer and started heading back towards her.

Once there, I took up the seat on the swing next to her, throwing my arm over the top of the seat and looking up at the sky.

"I've got time," I added, placing the beer between my legs and staring at her.

She grimaced, then sighed.

"Well..." she cleared her throat. "It started when my best friend was raped."

I blinked, surprised at the course this story had taken.

"Yeah?" I asked. "What happened?"

"I had a friend whose man left her, but only after he sexually assaulted her first." She bit her lip. "She filed charges. The guy got off; his daddy had a lot of money and clout with a couple of judges," she said. "And Angelica started to slowly go into a downward spiral. One second she was this upbeat girl who volunteered at animal shelters, and the next she was in a depression so deep that she barely got out of bed."

My stomach sank.

"And she tried to commit suicide, but I got there in time to call an ambulance. They pumped her stomach, and then kept her on a psychiatric hold for forty-eight hours before releasing her again." She took a deep breath. "And I took it upon myself to help her get out of her funk."

"And how'd you do that?" I asked.

She smiled.

"I started to burn the guy's cars. When he'd get a new one, I'd take Angel over there with me, and we'd light the car on fire again," she grinned.

"And you got caught?" I guessed, taking a sip of my beer.

She shook her head.

"No," she admitted. "We went out to celebrate one night after his car was torched for a second time, this time not by me, but I made a mistake."

"What mistake?" I asked.

"I dropped my boyfriend/fiancé's lunch off for him, and caught him fucking his partner in his patrol car," she grimaced, her face a mask of embarrassment.

My mouth dropped open in surprise.

"That was *you*?" I asked.

She shrugged, and another boom of thunder sounded overhead.

I wanted to wrap both arms around her and tell her that I was sorry, that she didn't deserve to be treated like that, but I knew those words wouldn't help her.

Nothing would but time.

"So…by me going off the chain at the police station, there were about eight million cops as witnesses to my act, meaning I couldn't deny anything." She shook her head. "My brother did what he could, getting me house arrest and probation instead of jail time. Because fucking Danny pressed every charge he could."

"This is Danny Salazar?" I guessed. "Naomi's brother? The traffic cop that writes everyone tickets?"

She sighed, then nodded.

"One and the same." She rolled her eyes to the roof, letting the back of her head rest against my arm.

I don't think she realized she was doing it, but I sure did.

Jesus, my dick sure did pick an awesome time to wake back up.

I crossed one leg over the opposite knee, reaching my hand down and using my leg as cover to readjust my cock in my pants.

"I heard he's a dick," I mentioned, gauging her reaction.

She sighed, long and loud.

"He is. Most definitely," she agreed. "But his partner is an even bigger dick. I hated her for the longest time; and it hurts more, I think, to know that he cheated on me with *her*."

"Seems like good riddance to me," I muttered, only saying exactly what was on my mind.

I was forty-two years old.

I didn't mince words. Not anymore.

I told it how it was, sparing no one's feelings.

Which I think was another thing that took my daughter's affection from me.

She hated that I was no longer with her mom and made no attempt to hide the fact that she was mad at me.

She intentionally acted out in school, no doubt a ploy for attention. I called her out on it when I picked her up from school after she was sent home to start a mandatory, three-day suspension for her outburst.

And I hadn't seen her since.

It'd been three weeks.

"Where's your head at?" A soft voice asked from beside me.

I turned to study Aspen.

"My kid," I admitted.

"Your kid?" She repeated in surprise.

I nodded.

"How old is he?" She said, throwing her hair back over one shoulder.

"*She's* sixteen," I told her.

"Ohhh," she smiled. "That's a fun age. I remember when I was sixteen."

I regarded her closely.

"Why do you say it like that?" I asked suspiciously.

"I lost my virginity at sixteen," she admitted. "And I was a bad girl. I partied more than I slept."

I glared at her.

"That's not what I want to hear," I told her. "I'm already dreading meeting her first boyfriend."

"What if she's already had one for a year now?" She teased.

I pinched her thigh, causing her to laugh.

"No, really. I was a good girl. I didn't lose my virginity until I was twenty-two," she decreed. "And even then, I wouldn't count it as losing my virginity."

"Why?" I asked curiously.

I didn't like thinking about her being with another man, and I hadn't even been with her yet.

Yet.

Thunder boomed and a streak of lightening had me laughing when Aspen jumped.

I lifted the beer, still cold from the just above freezing temperature outside, to my lips and took a long sip.

My throat worked as I swallowed nearly all of it in less than thirty seconds.

"You're pretty good at that," she observed.

"You're avoiding the question," I evaded, dropping the bottle down until the frozen bottom rested against my erection.

I pressed down slightly, hoping to relieve the throbbing that was still there, but it didn't work. Especially when I watched Aspen lick her lips and run the tip of her finger along the top of her knee.

Who knew that sweat pants would do it for me?

I sure as fuck didn't.

And they weren't even nice. You could tell that they were years upon years old.

Plus, I was fairly sure she was no longer a 'Bulldog.'

"He finished before he could get all the way inside me," she snapped. "Happy?"

I nodded.

Immensely.

Thunder boomed once again and I sighed, getting up but being sure the beer bottle hid the majority of my erection from her face, especially since it was now on eye level with her.

"I'm gonna go get my wood inside so it can dry out some," I told her. "It's supposed to flood, which'll inevitably knock the power out, and then I'll be freezing my balls off."

She stood, too, toe-to-toe with me, our feet just barely a foot apart.

"Thanks for helping," she said. "I already feel better."

"They only kept your friend overnight because they were worried about her concussion," I told her. "She should be out by tomorrow."

Aspen held up a thumb. "Good."

I grinned at her, touching the tip of her nose with my beer bottle before backing up and turning, heading down the steps.

"Hey!" She called.

I stopped and turned back to her.

"What?" I asked, attempting to shield my crotch so she wouldn't see the way my work slacks tented in the front.

"What's your name?" She asked.

I grinned.

"Drew."

She held up her thumb again.

"Cool."

CHAPTER 5

Fuck. Fucker. Fuckity fuckwad.
-Aspen's secret thoughts

Aspen

I was officially freezing.

Was it possible to get frostbite in less than an hour?

That's how long the power had been out.

Drew's prediction had come true.

He'd said that the power would go out, and it had.

I just wished I had been able to prepare for it.

Even now, I had two blankets on top of me, but if it got too much colder, I'd literally start crying.

The battery operated emergency clock/thermometer I'd pulled in from the garage read forty-nine degrees, and I was cursing myself for my stupidity.

I'd already had it set at sixty-two due to the fact that I could barely afford the bills as it was, and now it was reflecting how cold it was outside seeing as there hadn't been much heat to begin with.

"Mother of pearl," I whined. "This is the worst month ever!"

A knock sounded at my door, and I opened it to find my brother on the other side.

"What?" I snapped.

He narrowed his eyes at me.

"I need your help," he said.

"With what?" I asked.

"I was called into a SWAT call, and I need you to watch my kids," he explained.

"I can't," I told him. "I have no power."

"They like playing with flashlights," he shrugged.

"It's too cold," I reiterated. "It's already forty-nine degrees in here. There's no way I'll be able to get your kids to stay under blankets."

"Then start a fire," he tried.

"I don't have any wood," I continued, a little peeved now.

He growled in frustration.

"It's for ten minutes, at most," he threw up his hands. "Just wrap them up, and they'll be fine."

Four hours later and he still wasn't back.

I looked over at my brother's babies.

They sure were adorable.

Sighing, I reached over and turned on the music, smiling when my favorite song came on.

I sang along quietly with Garth Brooks, trying hard not to wake the kids.

The low gas indicator dinged, and I winced.

I'd been in my car for a good three hours now, scared as hell that if I left them inside they'd freeze and get hypothermia.

I was using the car as a charger anyway.

All of my tablets that I read on for work, as well as my phone and computer, were currently plugged into every electrical outlet or cigarette lighter in the car.

The gas indicator dinged again, and I bit my lip.

I sure wished I could actually drive my car. I'd take the kids over to my mom's place.

Not that I had any car seats, but the neighbor next door let me use her spares when I needed to go pick the kids up from daycare on the rare occasion that Downy let me have them.

Not that I knew her number, and I wasn't allowed to go into her yard anymore, so it was all a moot point.

I closed my eyes, ignoring the way the gas indicator dinged again, and fell into a light sleep.

And woke up what felt like seconds later, but was probably more like an hour or more.

The car was cold again, and the kids were still bundled up sleeping in the backseat.

I turned my head, smiling at not just my brother's wife, Memphis, but Drew as well.

Instead of losing what heat was left in the car and rolling the window down, I pushed the door open and quickly closed it.

"Hey," I said breathlessly.

"I'm so sorry," Memphis, apologized, throwing her arms around me. "I couldn't get off, and Downy's at a stupid SWAT call still."

"Gonna be a couple of hours or more," Drew offered his thoughts.

I furrowed my brows.

"How do you know?" I asked.

He held up his handheld radio to me.

"I'm listening to it," he wiggled the radio. "They've got a man that refuses to come out of his house, and he's holding his family hostage."

It was then I took in his attire.

"Why are you dressed in SWAT clothes?" I asked in alarm.

He was a firefighter, wasn't he?

I wasn't lusting after some cop, was I?

I couldn't do another cop. Not after what Danny had done to me. So all the time I'd been having certain thoughts about a certain firefighter had been a lie! He *was* a cop. Well, sort of. SWAT team meant cop, didn't it?

A chill swept over me.

"I'm a medic on the SWAT team," he explained. "I wasn't needed yet, since they weren't going in, and Memphis couldn't find you and called Downy. I was sent."

I blinked.

"I have an ankle monitor," I pointed to the offending thing that made all my clothes look funny at that ankle. "Why would you think I was anywhere else but home? There would be cop cars here by now if that was the case."

Memphis looked sheepish.

"I'm afraid that was my fault," she explained. "I couldn't get into your house because it's locked, and you weren't answering the door. I forgot my phone, but I had the radio in my car, and I called into dispatch."

My mouth dropped open.

"You're allowed to do that?" I asked.

She nodded…then shrugged.

"Maybe not," she said with a smile. "Probably gonna hear about it tonight, but there was no way I was going to leave and then come back. Not with how bad these roads are."

She indicated to the road behind her, showing me the snow-covered roads.

"Oh, okay." I nodded. "Well, they're in my car."

Memphis nodded, opening the backdoor.

"I'll bring the blankets back to you, if you don't mind," she said.

I was about to tell her that was one of my three blankets—yes, only three to my name—but then I saw the instant she opened the door, and realized it was too cold out there for her kids to go without. Sighing in frustration, I told her to take them.

"You can have them," I agreed.

"No," she said, shaking her head. "I'll get Downy to drop them back on his way home from work."

I nodded.

"Okay," I breathed a sigh of relief.

Then again, it wasn't like I needed an excuse to get onto Amazon. My finger was already getting itchy.

However, my bank account told me how stupid that'd be.

Luckily, my blog's royalty check would be coming in soon.

Not to mention my advertising check, so I *should* be fine.

But until I could get paid, I'd be down a blanket that I couldn't replace until at least two weeks from now.

"I'll take him," Drew offered.

Memphis smiled, handing Lock over, thankfully.

Lock was three, but he was a hefty forty-something pounds. I'd noticed when I'd taken him to the car from the house.

Their baby, Ares, who wasn't so much a baby anymore at a year and a half, was about half the size of her brother. She also had her daddy's red hair, which made me smile when the only thing you could see poking out of the blanket were her fiery red curls.

"Thanks again, Aspen," she thanked me softly.

My heart smiled at how much I liked my sister-in-law.

It wasn't her fault she was married to an ogre.

An ogre that I loved with all my heart.

"Be careful," I ordered her.

She smiled, kissed my cheek, and was gone a few moments later.

Drew waved at me from the driveway where he'd put Lock into Memphis' car, and I waved back.

Then I went back inside, grateful I had a gas oven I could turn on, and sat in front of it, leaning against my kitchen island, with my lone blanket.

I was also cursing myself for not getting the rest of my stuff out of storage.

I'd moved into this new house about three months ago, and I had plenty of time to get it done, yet I hadn't gotten around to doing it.

"Damn," I said, shivering slightly as the warm started to fill the room. "I forgot my computer."

Heaving a sigh, I got up once again, grabbed my laptop and the other electronics I'd spent the time charging, and then got to work on typing up tomorrow's blog post.

This one was titled: *The reasons one needs five tablets.*

Number one on the list was in case you were reading and the first one ran out of juice in the middle of it.

The second was in case of power failure.

The list went on, and I smiled for the first time since Memphis and Drew had left.

At least I was able to smile, so not everything could be as bad as I thought, right?

Lani Lynn Vale

CHAPTER 6

Nothing's ever as bad as it seems. Unless you lost a finger, then it's pretty bad.
-Drew's thoughts while working

Drew

"Your sister had to get into her car with our kids, Downy," I heard Memphis say over the speaker on his phone. "And now I feel like crap because I took two of her blankets. I need you to drop them back off to her for me. You'll have to come home to get them."

"Why don't I just go buy her new ones?" Downy asked distractedly. "And why was she in the car?"

"You were the one who told me her power was off and she didn't have any firewood. I would guess it was because she thought they were cold," Memphis growled at her husband.

I looked at Downy, then back to the camera that was being threaded through the first bedroom's vent in the house where a father was currently holding his family of five hostage.

He was holding them in the very middle of the house, in a tiny room with no windows or doors other than the one that led into the hallway.

He had enough guns to arm a small militia in there with him, too.

"I want you to bring her some firewood, too," Memphis continued. "And some food."

"Memphis...," Downy started.

"Downy, I'm not kidding here. She's lost weight in the last week."

Had she?

I hadn't noticed.

But then again I'd only met her last week, so I didn't have much to go by.

"I'll get it to her tomorrow," Downy started.

"No," Memphis snapped. "You'll do it today, or I'll go do it myself when you get home."

Downy growled in frustration, but then leaned forward as the camera finally made it to the room where we thought the family was being held.

The only thing we had to go on was one single phone call to 9-1-1 four hours earlier saying that their 'father' was holding them hostage and they couldn't leave.

"Gotta go," Downy said. "I'm busy."

He hung up on Memphis' growl of frustration.

"You know you're going to have to do that, right?" I asked.

"Yes," he sighed. "You live across the street from her, you should do it."

My eyebrows rose.

"She's right, you know," I said. "You owe it to her."

"How do you figure?" He asked, leaning forward at the same time I did.

"She watched your kids for four hours and used the last of the gas in her car to keep them warm. And your wife took her blankets when she has no heat. How do you not see that you owe her?" I asked somewhat irritated in his flippant behavior.

"Four hostages," Luke, the SWAT leader on scene, and all around good guy, said. "He doesn't have any guns on him."

"I don't even see any in the room," Nico, another member of the SWAT team, offered.

"Let's do this."

Then we went to rescue the hostages, who were being held at dick point. And by dick point, I meant his dick was out, and he was refusing to let them go without a fight.

***

I was just getting home, having being held over due to a report I had to write and fax in since I wouldn't be working for the next few days.

I'd requested the days off so I could spend some time with my daughter before she went back to school after Christmas break, but it was very clear by the end of the day when Attie still hadn't answered my messages or returned my phone calls that I wouldn't be getting any father/daughter time for the next few days like I'd planned.

I slipped and slid my way home, annoyed that I hadn't gotten around to putting new tires on my truck like I'd intended to this week.

Now I could barely get any purchase, and my four-wheel drive was practically useless seeing as the treads on my tires were nearly nonexistent.

I felt the first smile I'd cracked in over six hours moving across my face when I pulled into my driveway and saw Downy pulling to the curb.

His truck was loaded down with wood, nearly a whole cord would be my guess.

He dropped out of his truck gingerly, and then a dark missile of fur darted out right behind him.

"I told you to stay in the truck!" Downy boomed as he yelled at his dog, Mocha.

Mocha didn't spare him a glance as she ran to the front steps, then barked loudly at the door until Aspen finally opened it for her.

Mocha darted in, and Aspen immediately closed the door behind her.

"Your sister likes your dog more than she likes you," I observed dryly as I came around the back of my truck.

Downy flipped me off.

"Come help me with this shit," he ordered. "My power just went out, and I don't want to leave them there by themselves for long."

I didn't mention the fact that he'd had no problem leaving the kids with his sister in exactly the same conditions, but I had a feeling it had more to do with his wife being cold that was the reason for his urgency.

We worked for nearly twenty minutes in silence to get the wood to the side of the house, and the last fifty pieces or so went right outside Aspen's backdoor.

Then, without another word, he walked up the front walk, and straight inside her house, leaving the door open as he went.

"Aspen!" Downy called from inside the house.

I followed, almost out of curiosity rather than need.

I followed the sound of growling to the kitchen where I saw Downy facing off with his dog.

"Sit," Downy ordered.

The dog backed up, protecting the muffin in her mouth.

"Drop it," he said fiercely.

Mocha stared at him, then promptly tossed it up in the air, caught it, and swallowed it nearly whole.

"You shit head," Downy said. "How'd she even get that?"

"She brought it in with her. I tried to get her to let me have it, but as soon as I got the packaging off it she ate it," Aspen said.

I couldn't listen to them bitching anymore, though. Not with Aspen's legs only inches away from the open oven door.

"Can you please close that," I said. "You're going to burn yourself."

Then, almost as if in a movie, she whipped around.

The bottom of her sweater whirled out behind her, and I swear I watched as the damn thing caught fire as the end of it grazed over the burners on top of the stove.

Her sweater went up so fast that the only thing I could do was tackle her to the ground.

I hit her hard, and her body slammed to the floor under mine.

Almost instantly, I was up and off her, rolling her around, back-to-front, again and again.

"Shit!" Downy said, dropping down to his knees beside us.

I moved completely off of Aspen, rolling her over so I could see her face.

"You okay?" I asked her.

She nodded, dazed, her head the only thing that moved.

"You're sure?" I asked.

She nodded again.

"Can you breathe?" Downy asked laughingly, poking Aspen in the side. "He took you down like a linebacker does a quarterback."

"You suck," she replied through a wheeze, rolling over to her back, then getting her knees under her.

The sweater was a goner.

Her ass, though, looked to be perfectly fine.

Very fucking fine.

I licked my lips as the leggings she was wearing stretched tight over her ass as she pushed up to her hands and got to her feet.

I got up right after she did, watching to see if she'd fall or not.

Once I was sure she wouldn't, I moved over to the oven, closing the door and turning off the burners, before I turned and left the room.

I got firewood from the front porch, stacked ten pieces next to the fireplace, and then went about starting a fire.

I had to laugh when I pulled out a box of paper plates, cups, and napkins that were being stored in the fireplace.

Then laughed even harder when I pulled out what appeared to be a teddy bear.

Once everything was safely removed, I turned the gas on and lit a paper plate, thrusting it into the fire.

As the paper burned, igniting the wood, a fire was roaring quickly.

"Where'd all that come from?" Aspen asked, pointing at all the stuff I'd removed from the fireplace.

"That looks like Lock's," Downy pointed to the now very dirty bear before stooping down to pick it up. "I left your groceries on the front porch."

Aspen smiled, and we both watched as he stomped out of the house, Mocha hot on his heels.

We both looked at each other.

"You want to stay for dinner?" She asked softly.

I studied her face, as well as the hands she hadn't stopped ringing since I'd gotten there.

"What are you cooking?" I teased.

It'd take some near excellent cooking to get me to stay.

I was fucking tired, and the only thing that might keep me up longer than twenty minutes was a good, hot meal.

"I can make anything in the freezers." She offered.

I looked at the fire behind us, then back at her face.

"Okay," I said.

"Great!" She cried excitedly. "Do you want baked chicken or taco soup?"

"Chicken," I replied instantly.

She grinned, then walked around the door and hurried into the kitchen, her sweater gone.

"You might want to change your shirt!" I yelled at her, just now realizing that it had a sizable hole.

Her horrified gasp had me smiling, but it was her anger at having her most 'favorite shirt ever' ruined that had me laughing.

"Shut up!" She cried loudly. "They don't make these anymore!"

I rolled my eyes, tossing another piece of wood onto the fire before I picked up one of the blankets Downy had tossed back onto the couch and followed her.

I studied her kitchen as I waited for her to return.

It was on the newer side of old, but, like my place, it was definitely in need of some tender, loving care.

Aspen came back into the room, a look of sheer annoyance on her face as she practically waddled into the room, a heavy winter cloak covering her body from mid-thigh up.

"You want this?" I asked her once she came back in the kitchen.

She looked at me, held up her hands, and gestured to the blanket.

"What, you don't like this?" She indicated the jacket.

I grinned, then studied it.

"It looks like one of those jackets you get at the Ice Place in Dallas," I said. "Did you steal it?"

She shook her head.

"No," she said. "Not... *exactly*."

I snorted.

"They had those out at Disney on Ice. And they make you pay for it if you don't give it back," I said.

"That's true," she said. "But I stole it from the ex. He bought it for his ex, but he never gave it to her."

I snorted.

"That's a lie," I said. "He probably just didn't want to hear you bitching about wearing another girl's clothes."

She pursed her lips, then shook her head.

"I'm not contemplating that right now," she ignored me. "Now move over so I can get into the freezer."

I moved, leaning my hips against the counter, unfolding the blanket.

Once I'd wrapped it around myself, I watched as she practically disappeared into the large deep freezer.

"When I got on house arrest," she chattered. "Naomi brought me a shit ton of meat and staples," she said from somewhere deep in the freezer. She emerged long moments later with her hands full of foil pans. "And I sat down and made a shit ton of freezer meals."

"That's convenient," I murmured.

My cell phone vibrated, and I pulled it out without looking at the display.

"Hey do you want…" I held up my finger and then put the phone to my ear.

"Hello?" I answered.

"Who was that?" My daughter asked rudely.

I rolled my eyes to the ceiling and raised my hand so I could pinch the bridge of my nose.

"That would be my neighbor," I said. "How are you, baby?"

"There isn't any school tomorrow, and I was wondering if you could give me a ride to the mall," Attie said snottily.

I looked out the kitchen window, saw that the snow was still coming down, and promptly said, "No."

"Why not?" She challenged.

"Because you don't need to be going out in this. Nobody knows how to drive in it, and I don't see any reason to risk your life so you can go shop at the mall."

"Mom said I could," Attie snapped.

"Well, your mom," I said patiently. "Doesn't work in the emergency services field. She's a checker at the grocery store two doors down from your house. She doesn't see what I see when the roads get bad and people unnecessarily travel on them."

My daughter, my sweet baby girl, had developed a deep seated hate for me, and I didn't know why.

And this rude, mean thing wasn't my kid.

This was Constance's doing.

Constance was a pain in my fucking ass, as well as being very high maintenance. She also had that poor, pitiful me attitude.

There were times, like right now, that I wanted to point to this person she'd turned our daughter into so I could show her how stupid she was.

Still is.

When I'd been there, Attie had been a wonderful, sweet, caring little girl.

Now she was…whatever the hell she was.

Annoying was what I liked to call it.

"I hate you," Attie promptly hung up.

"Well, that went well," I muttered darkly.

I looked up to find Aspen's eyes on me.

They didn't look sad or even sympathetic. They looked almost aggravated. *Angry.*

"Was that your ex?" She asked.

I shook my head.

"No," I pushed my phone back into my pocket. "That was my daughter."

"Your daughter said she hated you?" She gasped.

"Yep."

CHAPTER 7

To really get to know a person, you should get them to use a computer with dial-up internet to get a good judge on their character.
-Aspen's secret thoughts

Aspen

Dinner had been nice.

I'd burned it a little bit, but as long as you didn't scoop too deep, it was fine.

What wasn't fine, however, was the way Drew was still...sad.

He looked almost defeated since his daughter had phoned.

"Do you want to play cards?" I wiggled my brows.

He looked at me strangely.

"What kind?" He held out his hand.

I handed him the deck, and he grinned at the picture of my cat that was on the front of it.

"Those are cute," he grinned.

I nodded.

"They are. I got them for free," I informed him. "I'm a product tester. My blog is a women's lifestyle blog. I discuss everything from romance novels to consumer products aimed at women. I have a pretty large following, and I kind of got into product testing, now, too."

"Like what?" He wondered. "What was the weirdest thing you ever tested?"

I pursed my lips.

"I get weird things all the time," I pursed my lips. "But the most recent one was this little device that allows women to pee standing up."

His mouth twitched.

"How'd that work out?" He wanted to know.

I shrugged.

"I read some previous reviews, luckily, and tried mine out in the shower the first time. However, the first time I tried to use it while wearing pants, I ended up peeing all over myself," I admitted. "Which was one of the things I mentioned in my review."

"Do you still use it?" He asked, shuffling the cards loudly.

I shook my head. "No," I admitted. "I don't have much use for it. I've never gone anywhere that didn't have a restroom."

"Never?" He asked.

I shook my head. "Never."

"Not hunting?" He wondered.

Another shake of my head.

"Nope," I said. "Dad was a little busy with his empire, and I didn't rate on his scale of people that he wanted to spend time with."

"When's the day you get out of your prison?" He indicated the walls of my house.

"I have two more months before they'll review my case for early release. It's kind of like being on a probationary period for probation," I sighed. "Then I get re-evaluated, and if I'm a good girl, I might get released. I was told that early release rarely ever happens, though. So it's likely that I will have five more months."

I nodded. "I sometimes want to put one of those on my daughter."

I shot him a look.

"Don't," I blurted. "This is the best time of her life and she doesn't even realize it. She'll forever have these memories to fall back on…to wish that this time in her life was still her present instead of her past." I continued. "When I was sixteen, I had the best of all worlds. My brothers loved me. My parents loved me. I was sheltered from everything that could ever do me harm. All my bills were paid, and the only thing I had to worry about was what to wear to school the next day that would make my boyfriend want to kiss me."

He shuddered. "I don't want to think about my daughter kissing anyone."

I laughed.

"You know she's most likely already done that, if not even more," I observed dryly.

He shot me a look.

"Take it back," he ordered.

I laughed at him.

"You're deluding yourself if you think those thoughts haven't crossed her mind," I teased.

"She's fifteen!" He boomed furiously. "She shouldn't be having those kinds of thoughts."

"I thought you said she was sixteen," I challenged him.

"She isn't…yet. She will be in six days," he muttered under his breath.

"So she's sixteen," I told him. "And she's not just going to randomly sleep with guys. If she's anything like most sixteen-year olds, she'll have her first sexual experience, realize it's not as great as it was made out to be, then never really think about it again."

He shot me a dirty look, knowing I was lying.

I held my hands up in peace.

He then quickly changed the subject…sort of.

"So you're telling me your *real* first experience was that horrible?" He asked carefully.

I grimaced.

"Yes," I said, nodding my head for emphasis. "It was so horrible, in fact, that I cried for nearly four hours afterward."

"Why?" He pushed, stretching his legs out in front of him in front of the fire.

The move put his arm along the back of the couch where my shoulders rested, and I felt a shiver run up my spine when his hot skin brushed the skin of my neck.

"The usual, I guess," I shrugged. "I was a virgin. He was big and didn't care that I was inexperienced. He pretty much used me."

He grumbled something under his breath.

"What?" I asked.

"I said not everyone with a big cock acts like that asshole did," he said more clearly this time.

My eyes widened as he turned away, studying the fire in front of us.

Did he have a big cock, I wondered?

My eyes went to his lap, but the blanket that was bunched up at his waist didn't really give me the best of views.

"No," he answered my question.

"No what?" I questioned.

"Nothing," he muttered.

"Tell me!" I ordered him.

I was a persistent devil, if nothing else.

He looked over at me, studying my expression, then grinned before shrugging.

"I'll tell you if you tell me..." he said.

"Tell you what?" I asked. "I don't have a cock, big or small."

He shuffled the cards in his lap before dealing out an even hand to the both of us.

"Let's play War," he taunted.

I laughed in his face.

"Ok, that's fine," I repositioned myself. "But what was it you wanted me to tell you?"

He opened his mouth, closed it, looked around, then looked back at me.

"I'll tell you whether I have a big cock or not like you are wondering, if you tell me about your worst sexual experience, and you can't count high school."

My jaw nearly hit the floor.

Or at least my boobs.

"What?" I asked in outrage. "I wasn't wanting to know that!"

He gave me a look, and my blush gave me away.

"Sorry," I muttered. "but I'm not usually so forward with people I don't know really well."

He snorted.

"You think I go around bargaining to tell people about my cock to get them to tell me something?" He laughed.

I shrugged.

"I don't know you all that well, do I?" I asked. "You could be getting all the girls to be your friend, and then you start threatening to tell them about your dick and get them all weirded out."

He muttered something under his breath, and I sighed, crossing my legs, as I flipped the first card in my stack over.

He flipped his first card over, and I growled when he won the first hand.

"Does your telling me about your dick come with a story?" I challenged him, causing his eyes to come up to mine.

His eyes were so beautiful.

They were a light shade of gray with a ring of a color I hadn't quite decided yet. Maybe green…or blue. In different lighting, it looked like the color changed.

I hadn't gotten the chance to study him too closely yet due to the power being out, despite spending nearly four hours in each other's company.

"If you want," he acquiesced.

His blonde hair reflected the color of the fire, making it appear reddish blonde when it was in fact graying blonde.

"Okay," I hummed. "My worst sexual experience?"

He nodded.

I grinned.

"Danny had to take a little blue pill for the majority of our relationship if he wanted to get hard," I admitted. "So then he'd last for hours, and I hated having sex with him."

He blinked. Slowly.

"That's it?" He wondered.

I nodded. "His cock was, I don't know, just weird. It was shaped like a banana. It was skinny, and it was really curved. Something about it… it was just ugly, ok? And even worse was that he didn't know what to do with it. Ugh. It got to be that I dreaded having sex with him, it was starting to gross me out."

His mouth dropped open.

"Then why were you still with him?" He blurted in surprise. "And why the hell did you flip the fuck out and fuck his car up…and him?"

"I don't really know," I confessed. "He felt…safe. We didn't do it all that often, and now that I know why, it's not as soothing as it once had been. Danny and I were really good friends before he asked me out, and it's hard to lose ten years of friendship."

"So you stayed with him out of obligation, and because you didn't want to lose his friendship," he rumbled.

I shrugged. "Yeah, I guess."

He gave me a look.

"Why'd he do this to you? Treat you like that? Take all your things when he left?" He pushed. "You're not telling me everything."

I bit my lip, wondering if I should tell him the next part.

"I wanted to get married, to have kids," I finally explained. "Lots of them. I'm already pushing thirty. He just seemed like my safest bet to get that."

Something flashed in his eyes so fast that I couldn't read it before it was gone, but it definitely had me intrigued.

"My cock's considered large. And on a scale of large cocks, it's on the larger side," he changed the subject.

My eyes flicked to his lap again, but the blanket was still in the way.

His chuckle brought my eyes back to his.

"I'm sorry," I said honestly. "But you can't just say something like that and not expect me to look."

His smile had flutters erupting in my belly.

"I'll have to remember that for next time," he said. "I win."

I looked down at the cards between us, all of which were now on Drew's side of the invisible line, and I cursed.

"Cheater."

He shrugged. "I'm older and know more tricks. Cheating in cards is relative. It's more like knowing all the ways to play the game."

CHAPTER 8

Why bother spraying Febreeze after you shit? All it does is make it smell like shitrus, not citrus.
-Text from Aspen to Naomi

Drew

So the nights at Aspen's house continued.

We were on day six of our fucked up winter storm.

I'd worked a double shift the two nights before, and today was the first time I'd seen her in nearly fifty hours.

I felt like a fucking juvenile. All I could think about was if Aspen was warm enough, or if she was keeping herself well entertained.

Then I'd pulled into my driveway to see a massive snowman in her yard the size of which I'd never seen in Texas.

The sign on the front of the massive snowman said, 'Do you want to build a snowman?'

I'd laughed all the way up her driveway, and when she opened the door and I'd smelled the bacon cooking, I'd come inside and hadn't left since.

"What's the worst thing you've ever done?" Aspen asked, egging me on.

I lifted my beer, the ninth or the tenth, and stopped when I realized it was empty.

"You want the truth?" I asked.

"We are playing truth or dare," she said, laughter filling her voice.

I shrugged.

"I was in college," I said, apologizing ahead of time for what I was about to tell her.

"Okay…" she said, looking at me out of the corner of her eye before taking another swig of her bottle.

She passed it over to me, and I took a drink of her wine.

"I thought you said you weren't allowed to have alcohol," I said after I took a long swig.

"I'm not." She took another swig. "But it's either I drink, or I run away. I think drinking is the better end of the spectrum."

I didn't argue with her. I just hoped they didn't randomly show up and test her.

That would suck.

Aspen giggled, causing my gut to clench even more tightly than it had been throughout the day.

God, the way she laughed, so uninhibited, was so sexy.

In fact, the woman had a way of making me feel things I'd never experienced before in all my forty-two years of life.

Just by *laughing*.

"When I was in college, my roommate used to always come in and steal my stuff. Nothing was sacred. My clothes. My shoes. My food. My deodorant." I took another swig of the wine and passed it back. "Then, one day, I came in to half of my tube of toothpaste gone and I just…snapped."

Her eyes widened so far that it was almost comical.

"What did you do?" She pushed.

I closed my eyes.

"Did you just blush?" She asked.

I started to laugh.

"I'm not proud of myself," I admitted. "Now that I'm a firefighter, I realize how terrible bodily fluids are to share, but then…" I shook my head. "I was well and truly pissed, so I masturbated into a Ziploc bag and then squeezed it all into the toothpaste tube."

Her mouth dropped open.

"You didn't," she said, almost sounding envious.

I nodded again.

"I did," I winced. "And I felt terrible about it after it was all said and done," I told her. "I forgot about the toothpaste, having put it in a drawer and never looked back at it again," I smiled slightly at the memory. "Then one day I happened to glance in the drawer to find it nearly all the way gone, and I wrote my roommate a note."

"What did the note say?" She leaned forward, listening intently.

She was now on her knees, waiting for me to finish the story.

"I said, 'It's wrong to steal, and I don't appreciate your using my stuff without asking first. I hope you enjoyed brushing your teeth with my jizz in your toothpaste over the last month'," I admitted.

She gagged, slapping her hand over her mouth before she rolled over onto her side and started laughing uproariously.

I watched her roll around the floor on her back, tears coming down her cheeks as she laughed too hard to control her bodily functions.

"That's…" she wheezed. "Epic."

"What about you?" I asked her.

"Truth?" She said, raising her brow in question.

I nodded, practically vibrating with the desire to hear her answer.

"It's not really funny like yours. Mine's my worst shame. I have nightmares about it," she sighed softly.

I looked down at her, purposefully letting her see my disappointment, and then nearly laughed when she sighed so exaggeratingly.

But what I expected to be funny, was anything but.

I could've guessed just about anything would've come out of her mouth than what did.

"I'm not my father's kid," she whispered darkly.

My mouth dropped open.

"And that's a shame to you…how?" I wondered.

She bit her lip.

"If I tell you this…you have to promise not to tell anyone, *ever*," she ordered fiercely. "You cannot ever tell. If you tell, I'll probably be disowned by my mother, and I love her so much that I'd probably kill myself."

I blinked.

"If it's that big of a deal…" I started. "Then I don't want to know."

She waved me off.

"Downy's father died before I was born…" she started.

I nodded.

I'd heard that in our previous talks.

"Okay," I circled my finger for her to continue.

She bit her lip.

Then she opened her mouth and said words that I would've never expected to come out of her mouth.

"I'm not Downy's half-sister. I'm his full sister," she blurted.

I blinked.

"Ummm," I asked in confusion. "How?"

She got up and ran to her bedroom, then came back a couple minutes later with some documentation in her hands.

"Out of spite, one day when I was eighteen or nineteen," she started. "I got really mad at Downy, and I was going to prove to him once and for all that we weren't related."

I nodded.

"Don't ask why, I was a kid," she ordered.

I held up two fingers in a scout's honor.

She gave me a dirty look that clearly told me she'd fuck me up if I ever thought about telling.

"So I steal some of his hair, and then sent some of my hair in, to have it analyzed." She handed me the paperwork.

"What's this?" I asked, looking at the lines, dashes, and percentages.

"Okay," she took a deep breath. "This right here shows the likelihood of me being related to him."

She pointed to a number.

It read: *99.99%.*

My mouth dropped open.

"That's impossible unless…"

She was nodding before I had a chance to finish.

"Exactly," she said. "So I started to dig. I hired a private investigator to find out how. After running the test two more times."

"How, at eighteen, were you able to afford this?" I questioned.

She shrugged.

"My parents are wealthy, and when I turned eighteen, a small inheritance hit my account. I blew through it so fast my head spun, and I only have a few things to show for it," she sighed. "Anyway, so I have this man trying to figure out why, and when he comes to me with the news that I was conceived through artificial insemination from a sperm bank out of Dallas, it all started to make sense."

"So they froze your father's…sperm."

She nodded again emphatically. "That's what I think, anyway."

"And have you ever figured anything else out about it, or did you stop once you'd gotten that far?"

She shook her head.

"That's the shameful part of all this. I went through a hundred and fifty thousand dollars trying to figure it out…but I'd gotten shafted by the PI. He'd taken me for a naïve girl, and I had been," she admitted.

I shook my head.

"That's ludicrous."

She agreed with a grunt.

"But I count it as worth it…*to know*. I just wish I could have more information without bringing it up to my mom. This would break her for sure," she whispered, picking at invisible lint on her shirt.

A shirt that was clinging to her breasts like a fucking second skin.

My eyes jerked up to her face, and I breathed a sigh of relief when I saw she wasn't paying attention to where my eyes were aimed.

She was too busy looking at the fire.

Her hands wringing in her lap as she thought about what she'd just told me.

"What is it?" I asked.

She shook her head.

"I want to tell Downy, but I'm scared he'll tell my mom. Then my father will leave," she hesitated. "Again. My mom—she tried to leave him once for doing some stupid shit when it came to Downy a few years ago—but she couldn't function. When he got done serving his sentence, she went back to him. This is the last thing they need right now—me making it harder than it needs to be."

"You're thinking like a kid," I told her. "Think like an adult. You deserve to know who your father is. Why are you so worried about your parents? They're adults, too."

She pursed her lips, thinking long and hard before she gave voice to the words that were just at the tip of her tongue.

"My father's what you would call…difficult," she finally settled on. "He's not the nicest person in the world, and he's just an okay father. Not great, but not the worst either. I wasn't beaten. I never wanted for anything. Not a day went by that I worried if I would eat the next day, and I always had a roof over my head and a place to sleep." She exhaled. "But he's mean. Very mean, and it's my mom who ends up taking the brunt of it if we do something that displeases him."

"Take it, how?" I wondered.

"Doesn't take her to the business functions he attends, which she loves. Doesn't allow her to go out with him at all, in fact. My mom's pretty needy and clingy. She's very emotional, and although she's the best mom in the world, she's high maintenance," she explained. "She's not the kind of woman who would make it on her own. She'd fall apart if my dad left her."

"Hmmm," I murmured. "Then I'll just have to bow to your experience with her. If you think she won't be able to handle it, who am I to argue?"

"I've been fighting with myself about telling my brother, but …" She stopped when I held up a finger for her to hold on.

Pressing the green phone button, I answered my phone.

"Hi, Attie," I said. "How was your day off from school?"

She didn't bother to answer.

"You missed the pickup time," she grumbled loudly.

I looked at my watch and cursed.

"I'm sorry, honey. I thought we'd said we weren't doing it today because of the snow?" I said.

"And I told you," she said with not a little amount of attitude. "That I didn't want to reschedule."

I didn't argue with her. I'd figured out long ago that it was easier to just let the attitude go rather than confronting her about it.

"I'm sorry, pickle lily," I said softly. "Do you want me to come…"

She hung up, and I was left looking at the black phone like a dumbass.

"So…she sounds…nice," Aspen teased.

The corner of my mouth kicked up, and I stood, taking our plates and dishes to the trash.

"She's my baby, and I think she's trying to stay loyal to her mom without cutting me out of her life altogether. She doesn't really know how to balance that, and I think I get the brunt of it when she's on the phone. She doesn't do that when we're actually with each other. I think she puts that show on in front of her mom to make her feel better," I disclosed.

When I made it back to the living room, it was to find Aspen on her back next to the fire.

The orange flames cast a shadow throughout the room, and all over her body it looked like there was a soft orange glow playing across her porcelain white skin.

Skin that looked so soft that I wanted to rub my lips along her entire body just to see if it was as soft as I thought it might be.

My eyes drifted down the length of her body, stopping on the skull leggings that were covering her lower half.

My gaze caught on the apex of her thighs, and I nearly groaned when I saw how well those leggings hugged her pussy. I could almost see the outline of her pussy lips, and the seam that separated them.

I tore my eyes away from the tight pants and her pretty pussy, turning and gazing out the window in the living room.

My gaze fell on the house directly next door to mine.

"Is the house next to mine, the one with the green shutters, occupied?" I asked.

I'd never seen anyone there, but then again they could just have different hours than me.

That was possible.

I'd only been in the neighborhood for a short time period.

"That's Doris McQueen's house," she answered, curling up until she was standing. "That house is about to be foreclosed on, I think."

"How do you know?" I asked. "It looks deserted, but well kept."

"I saw them nail that pink sign on the door, which she then ripped off as soon as they left," she explained. "She's gonna be one of those people that stay there even when the wrecking ball is waiting outside, ready to knock the building down."

I snorted, my eyes going back to my house, then to the one on the other side of mine.

"What about the others," I pointed.

She stood up on her tiptoes, then moved in between me and the window as she tried to look over the car that I just now realized must be in her way.

And her ass rubbed against the tip of my cock, causing me to nearly jump out of my skin and jerk back a step in my haste to get away from her.

She looked behind me in confusion as she felt me abruptly pull away, but then turned around and looked back at the house next to mine.

"I don't know who that is," she said. "I've been watching this neighborhood for a while now, and I've never once seen anybody come in or out of that house. But someone has to be, because the paper is always picked up and so are the mail and packages. I just never see anyone doing it."

"Weird," I muttered, turning my back to her and walking back to the fire to stoke it, hoping during the couple of seconds it took for me to get it back up to life that my cock would learn how to control itself.

She knelt down on the floor, reaching under the coffee table and coming back up with the huge box I'd seen earlier.

"The mailman delivered this today," she said.

I blinked.

"The mailman?" I asked.

She nodded.

"Sure did," I said. "They had a tractor come down the road and clear the snow off, followed by a truck with some sand."

"Probably because this is one of the busier roads that everyone uses," I said. "I didn't realize they were getting off their asses to do anything today."

Her brows rose as she lifted the flaps on the box.

"I'm sensing some hostility there," she heckled.

I winced.

"The fire department, as well as the police department, has to run regardless of road conditions," I told her. "So it would've been nice for them to start doing that shit three days ago rather than today when it's finally clearing up."

"It's still raining," she said. "And is supposed to rain for the next week."

"It's supposed to rain, not snow. And that's a completely different thing," I said. "It's like comparing apples to apple pie. Same fruit, but one's more complicated than the other. And tastes better."

She snorted at the comparison. "I don't like apple pie."

I gasped in affront. "What kind of Southerner are you?"

She stuck her tongue out at me.

"Shut up," she sniffed. "Look what I got today."

I looked down into the box.

"What…is that?" I asked, staring at the tube filled with white powder.

"This," she lifted it. "Is a new product that I'm testing out."

I read the label and my jaw dropped open.

"That's…insane," I groaned. "What are you going to do with it?"

She grinned, showing a perfectly straight row of white teeth.

"This is where you come in."

And I had to add…had I not been on my second six-pack of beer, along with more than a couple long swigs of wine, I would've never considered doing it.

But I did.

And it was the best day of my life, ever.

***

Thirty minutes later, Aspen was a hot mess. Literally and physically.

"You should've never turned that battery powered heater on in here. I'm literally dying," she groaned, wiping sweat off her forehead with her elbows.

The heater was working well; I'd give her that.

It was something the boys at the firehouse had rigged up using a car battery. It put out a lot of heat and allowed me to sleep comfortably in my bed for the last week without having blankets piled a mile high on top of me.

I took a swig of my beer, well and truly buzzed now.

I couldn't even say how many I'd had at this point in the night.

A smile overtook my face when I realized I'd have to tell Luke, my boss on the SWAT team, that I couldn't come in if a callout were to happen right then.

I was well and truly *drunk*, and enjoying *every minute* of it.

"I'm going to be naked here in a few seconds," I said somewhat loudly, never able to control my mouth when I was this far gone. "You'll have to forgive me if I wanted to make sure there was no shrinkage. Have I mentioned that I can't believe I'm doing this right now?"

"Yes," she snickered. "About twenty times now. But it was your idea."

I snorted, then sat back on the counter in Aspen's bathroom.

"Okay," she grinned excitedly, looking at the thermometer in the water. "It's ready."

I crossed my arms over my chest.

"My cock needs inspiration," I said. "And it's only fair."

"What's only fair?" She sounded confused, leaning back to look at me, taking a swig from her bottle of wine while she did.

"I'm practically naked, and I will be in a few minutes. The least you could do is take your clothes off, too," I challenged.

I wasn't sure she was going to do it, but when she sat the bottle down onto the counter with a loud clunk, punctuating that sound by whipping off her shirt, I nearly swallowed my tongue.

She wasn't wearing a bra, meaning her perfectly formed, juicy breasts spilled out of her shirt, bouncing and swaying as she waited for my reaction.

My cock reacted instantaneously, rising up after nearly a year-long slumber.

"Holy fuck," I moaned, closing my eyes. "You should definitely put it back on."

I was nodding. Definitely. She needed to put it back on. *Now!*

If she didn't, I wouldn't be able to control myself.

I'd fuck her, and she'd let me.

It was as simple as that.

She gave me a knowing smile, glanced down at my cock, and then back to the water she'd just said came to the correct temperature.

"What does it say now?" She asked, indicating the directions I had in my hand.

"Pour the molding powder in," I told her.

She picked up the scissors, cut the bag open carefully, then poured it inside.

"Here," I said, handing her the spatula.

She took it with a small smile and started to stir.

I glanced down at the time on my watch, then back to her.

The movement of her arms as she stirred the pot had her tits swinging this way and that, brushing against her arm as she moved.

I stared studiously at my watch, staring hard until the thirty seconds were up.

"Okay," I said.

She stopped and waited for me to instruct her on her next step.

"Now pour it in the tube," I told her, reaching for the waistband of my underwear.

My cock popped free, and she faltered, staring in slack jawed surprise at my cock.

"Pour," I ordered. "Or it'll be too late."

She jumped like I'd pinched her and started pouring the mixture into the tube while looking back and forth between what she had in her hands and what I had in mine.

I stroked my cock while she watched, and I nearly came right then and there when she moaned as the bowl she was holding grazed the tip of her distended nipple, causing her body to jerk.

My hand reached out, almost as if it had a will of its own, and brushed the other neglected nipple.

Just a simple stroke of the backs of my fingers down the very tip of her breast.

By now, my cock was as hard as it'd ever been, and I was thinking that it might not ever return to normal, not with the way she was biting her lip and looking at me through hooded eyes.

I was seriously thinking there might actually be stretch marks along my cock come morning. I wasn't kidding about the fact that it was bigger.

As if it wasn't already big enough.

"Okay," she said, glancing down at my cock again. "Will it even fit in this tube?"

I shrugged.

I had no fucking clue.

We'd forgotten to measure the tube against my cock like the directions had said to do beforehand. I had no idea if it'd fit or not.

"I'm trying to figure out how to get it in there without spilling it. Do I, like, dunk it like a tea bag or something?" I asked, pointing at it, then at my cock.

"The YouTube videos I was able to find weren't very helpful. All they used were dildos, not actual cocks," she clarified.

I nodded, then got up, letting my underwear drop all the way to the ground as I did.

"Give it to me," I ordered, holding out my hand. "I'll try to lean over on the counter and point it down."

"No," she said. "You lean down on both elbows over the counter, and I'll get down here and...*guide it in.*"

So that was how I ended up with a hot, sweaty girl, her hands covered in white penis molding goo, at my feet with her hands on my dick.

I leaned over the counter, letting my cock hang heavily between my legs as I stared at her.

My raging hard-on started to throb to the beat of my heart, and she watched it intently as she reached for it.

I closed my eyes, unable to take the torture any longer.

And just when I was about to call the whole thing off, I opened my eyes to see her only millimeters from my cock.

She bit her lip, reaching forward to take my dick, and hesitantly pumped it twice, running her thumb over the tip before she inhaled deeply.

"They say sometimes it's better to use a cock ring," she whispered.

"Oh," I drawled. "I won't need a cock ring."

She looked up at me, then licked her fucking lips again.

"Do it," I growled through gritted teeth, my balls drawing up as she gave me one final pump, then guided my cock into the liquid goo.

As my cock slid into the tube, the white goop spilled over the sides onto the white tile floor of Aspen's bathroom.

It was such a weird sensation, almost like I'd dipped my dick into warm, partially set Jell-O. I don't know what to compare it to since my dick hadn't been dipped into anything other than a pussy, a mouth or a fist.

"I've got to say," I licked my lips, somewhat freaked out. "This is the weirdest thing I've ever felt."

She helped guide my heavy cock down until the tip of the bottle touched my pubic bone.

"God," she said. "You're touching the bottom, aren't you?"

I snorted, causing her to smack my bare ass. "Don't move!"

I didn't move.

Not for four long minutes as she slowly moved her hand up and down my backside.

I don't even think she realized she was doing it, either. I think she was just absently trying to offer me her support.

Or, at least, that's what I told myself.

Surely, she wasn't purposefully getting that close to my balls each time she swept her hands over and around me.

Two hundred and forty seconds later I choked out, "Time!"

My voice sounded like it'd been put through a shredder with how strangled it sounded coming out.

She pulled the casting off my cock so slowly, my eyes crossed at the suction.

And then I lost it.

The moment she had it off me and sitting on the counter, I reared up, grabbed the soap off the side of the counter, and furiously rubbed my cock and pubic hair with the soap.

Then I rinsed it off, making a mess of the floor and the counter in the process.

Once every smear of white goo was off my cock and pubes, I reached for Aspen and yanked her to me.

She hit my body hard, her gasp being captured by my mouth as I slammed my mouth down onto hers.

Somewhere in our fumbling she lost her pants and panties, and I growled in approval.

"Oh, God, yes," she gasped between kisses, jumping up and wrapping her legs around my hips.

Her ankle monitor dug into my ass cheek, but I didn't give a shit as I took her mouth with mine.

"You taste so good," I said, pulling back to look at her face.

She undulated her hips, rocking up and down, back and forth, letting the length of my cock become saturated in her juices.

"Condom," I moaned. "You got any in here?" I asked, placing my hand on the medicine cabinet currently holding her head up.

She shook her head.

"No," she moaned, licking her lips. "But I have some in that box in the living room."

I stepped back and she held on, wrapping her arms around me tight.

I held her by her ass as we walked out to the living room, my whole body shivering once the cool air of the rest of the house finally made itself known.

The living room, however, was nice and warm as I dropped down to my knees in front of the fire.

She let me go as she turned onto her side and reached into the box to pull out a few items.

Condoms.

Three different kinds.

Glow in the dark.

Flavored.

And ribbed.

"Which one?" She fumbled with the boxes.

"Who gives a fuck?" I held out my hand for one.

She rolled over onto her belly as she reached further into the box, coming up with a smaller box in her hand.

When she went to push up onto her hands and knees, I pushed her shoulders down.

"Stay down," I ordered, smacking her ass when she tried to rear up.

She complied, looking at me quickly as she ripped open the box.

Pulling a strip of squares out of the box, she tore one off and handed it back to me.

The rest of box's contents were littering the area and making it look like a fuckin' orgy was about to commence.

"Glow in the dark," she gasped, pushing her butt back against me as I ripped into the condom's wrapper, positioned it at the tip of my cock, and rolled the thing down my length.

Well…most of it, anyway.

There was still a good two inches left at the bottom of the condom.

"Did you buy the smallest size they had?" I asked her, reaching forward to grab her ass.

"No," she denied. "And I didn't buy them. They sent samples in exchange for an honest review."

My hands squeezed the supple flesh of her ass, massaging and kneading it as I tried to gain some semblance of control.

"Make sure you tell them that they're too small." I mumbled, touching the very tip of my now fluorescent green and glowing cock to her entrance.

"Too small, got it," she moaned, dropping her head and swaying her hips enticingly in my direction. "Normal sized people. Need bigger ones for your Incredible Hulk cock."

I made a low noise in the back of my throat in answer to that.

"Can you take a picture?" She asked.

I licked my lips.

Now, had I been completely sober, I would never had done something so crazy.

But I wasn't sober.

I was on my umpteenth beer, and who knows which glass of wine since we hadn't been using glasses.

A thump against my leg had me looking down to see her phone had dropped onto my foot, meaning I did what any irresponsible adult would do.

I took a fucking picture.

Of my green, glowing Incredible Hulk lightsaber dick.

Then I dropped the phone and lined my cock up with her entrance, slowly easing myself inside.

Thank fuck I went slow, too.

My eyes rolled back in my head at the feeling of how goddamned tight she was.

"Holy fucking hell," I squeezed out through a wheeze.

"Oh, my God!" She scrambled to her elbows. "I lied! I can't take it!"

I stilled her hips when she went to pull away.

"The wine made me courageous!" She cried, wiggling and making what little amount of cock I had in her scream in pleasure. "My vagina changed its mind!"

"Stay *still*," I said urgently. "Oh, fuck me you're so tight. *Stay still!*"

She wiggled and pushed, pulled and wiggled…and I kind of lost it.

But she kind of did, too.

I tried to pull back from her to sit on my heels. But she followed me, pushing down and, impaling herself almost fully onto my cock before she realized what she'd done.

I did the rest, pulling her to me until her back rested against my chest.

She let out a yelp that echoed through the living room.

"I can practically feel it in my throat," she moaned, her inner muscles working my cock as she adjusted to me.

"You have to stay still," I pleaded through clenched teeth, my eyes squeezed shut. "Please."

She growled and started circling her hips.

"It feels better now," she told me. "I can take you. I wasn't so sure I could."

I growled.

"You're fucking nuts," I swallowed, lifting her up by her hips and pulling her back down.

She moved with me, even going as far as shifting her legs to a squatting position giving me almost full control.

I pushed her up and pulled her down, causing her head to fall back and her long hair to brush my groin.

"My vagina and face are getting hot," she gasped. "I can't tell if it's because of the fireplace being right there, or because I'm so close to coming."

I chuckled against her throat, circling my arm around her hips to keep moving her up and down when she started to slow.

The other arm went to her pussy, my hands sliding down to cup where we were joined.

"Maybe a little of both," I told her, feeling how hot she felt.

I slowly started to move backwards on my knees, stopping when we hit the couch.

In an impressive show of strength considering my level of intoxication, I stood, holding her tight around her ribs, as well as continuing to cup her pussy.

My fingers split, going around the girth of my cock where it speared her entrance, resting along the soft, fleshy lips of her sex.

She whimpered at the sudden move, which took her feet completely from the ground.

She had no control whatsoever, then. I supported all of her weight, and she latched onto my forearms with her hands as the walls of her pussy gripped my dick. Her pussy was clenching around me so furiously, that I wasn't sure if I would ever get blood flow back in my dick.

"My feet aren't touching!" She gasped wildly. "Oh, holy shit."

I chuckled darkly, falling back onto the couch, which was as far as I was willing to go.

I didn't want to hurt her, which I might inadvertently do if I wasn't careful.

This being our first time, I sure as hell didn't want to mess up something that I knew I'd want to be inside of as much as I possibly could.

There was no way that I'd ever get enough of her pretty pussy.

Not when it felt this good.

"*Yesssss,*" she hissed, her knees pressing into the couch cushions as she leaned forward, bracing her hands on my knees as she started to bounce up and down.

I leaned back, my hands gripping the back of the couch while she started to go to town, using my cock and me as she worked herself into a frenzy all on her own.

I looked down, watching as the fireplace gave me just enough light to see that she was taking about three quarters of me inside of her with each downward thrust. Not to mention my dick still glowed.

I resisted the urge to grab her hips and slam her down all the way, worried that she was taking only what was comfortable for her.

But I must've thrust up a little more than I'd intended because she moaned, then started to slam herself down completely, her bottom resting against my legs before she moved back up my length.

I closed my eyes, pure bliss bubbling hotly through my veins as I started to count in my head.

I'd gotten up to three hundred before her pussy started to ripple.

I was at three fifty when she cried out her release, calling my name loudly as she did.

"Drew!" She screamed. "God, *yes!*"

I grabbed her hips then, unable to help myself as I pulled her down and thrust up simultaneously.

My growl filled the air as I came, long hard jets of semen leaving the end of my cock like a rifle shot.

My soul was nearly ripped out of my cock when her pussy clenched one last time, pulling the last dregs of my release with it.

"Jesus," she whispered, leaning back against me.

I absentmindedly ran my hands in a slow pattern, up and down, until our breathing returned to normal.

What didn't return to normal, though, was my cock.

"You're still hard," she whispered. "I thought older guys were supposed to have a problem getting it up."

I leaned forward and bit the back of her shoulder.

"I'll show you old," I said, pulling her off my cock, pulling off the too small condom, and tossing it onto the floor before I reached for the strip of condoms on the floor with my foot.

"This time you put it on," I ordered, pushing her forward.

She leaned forward, giving me a perfect view of her glistening, pink pussy, and I couldn't resist the urge to insert my finger where my cock had just been.

She was still tight, even after I'd taken her as hard as I did.

She gasped at the move, stilling as I worked my finger in and out, noticing how easily I slipped into her channel.

"You are so wet for me," I grated. "You want my cock back?"

She grunted in answer, drawing a smile from my lips.

"That a yes, baby?" I asked her.

Her pussy clenched on my finger.

I pulled it out, then immediately replaced it with two.

Her body fell back to the ground, her hands the only thing supporting her as I used my two fingers to fuck her.

Then two became three as I started to rub the head of my cock against her clit.

We were rocking in a nice little dance when she tossed the strip of condoms backwards over her shoulder, then went back to her hands.

"Please," she whimpered.

I took the condoms and ripped one off with my teeth and tore it open.

I withdrew my fingers from her to roll the condom on, this one red and even tighter than the one before.

I pulled her up off the floor, her hair falling back in a wavy sheet down her back as she let me move her where I wanted her.

My cock got pinned in between her body and mine as I stood once again, this time walking to the arm of the couch and turning her around to face me.

I nudged her belly with my hand until she sat, then gently pushed her back with the flat of my palm to the middle of her chest.

I took advantage of my hand's placement on her chest and swiped her nipple with the pad of my thumb as she fell backwards.

Her body bowed beautifully over the arm of the couch, putting her pussy in the perfect position for my cock.

I thrust into her in one fluid movement.

I stilled, enjoying the feeling of her speared on my cock, encasing me in her heat.

She once again took all of me, a feat not many women had been able to do.

I'd had maybe ten partners throughout my life, having mostly had long term relationships when I found someone I wanted.

And out of the ten, only two had been able to take all of me, but never the way Aspen did.

It wasn't like Aspen was well used or anything. It was like her body was made to take my cock.

She just fit me so perfectly, her walls wrapping me up snugly and sucking my entire length in. It was like two puzzle pieces snapping together.

I pulled my hand away from her chest and latched onto both of her hips, pulling nearly all the way out before I thrust back inside.

Her breasts bounced with the suddenness of the movement, her eyes slowly closing as she lost herself in the way I was making her feel.

Her sheath tightened around me as I steadily pumped into her, not stopping until long minutes later when she finally came apart around me.

Her hot pussy rippled, slowly sucking at my cock.

I looked down and watched my cock disappear inside of her, my gut clenching when I saw how full she looked.

With two more hard thrusts, my balls drew up, and I grunted in release as I followed her.

When the last drop left me, I slowly pulled out, only then noticing that the condom was no longer where it was supposed to be, which was on my cock.

I bit my lip as I pulled the condom from inside her with one finger, making her eyes go wide when she felt it leave her.

"You're shitting me right now, aren't you?" She gasped, doing some weird flip over her shoulder as she came to stand at my side, staring down in horror at the condom still in my hands.

Then she looked down at her thighs where my release was dripping down her left leg.

"I'm clean!" She blurted. "I had myself checked after Danny…you know."

I pulled her in by her hip, slamming my mouth down onto hers for a quick, hard kiss.

"I'm clean, too," I told her. "Had to get checked to join the SWAT team. Haven't had anybody since I left my ex a year ago."

"What about that chick I saw you with…the one that was there the night you helped me with my TV?" She asked hesitantly.

I shook my head. "Never went further than that kiss. Dinner and a kiss goodnight."

She pursed her lips, then her eyes caught on my side where a red, angry indention was raised up on my side.

"I think my ankle bracelet is dangerous," she whispered, running her fingers along the lines.

I chuckled then let her go, bending down to pick up the other used condom before tossing them into the fire.

"That's probably not the way you're supposed to dispose of those," she mentioned teasingly.

I shrugged.

"Make sure you write a review about that," I ordered her.

"About your performance, or the condom's performance?" She clarified with a little smirk.

"Both, honey. Let me know if you'd like to try anything else out."

She bent over the box and started pulling out sex toy after sex toy.

"Oh, I've got lots more to try out. How much time do you have?"

CHAPTER 9

Bitches be sippin'.
-Coffee Cup

Aspen

"I can't believe you had sex with him," Naomi stuttered. "Don't you have any shame?"

I turned my glare on her. "And if PD asked you right now if you would ride his kinky cock, you wouldn't?"

Naomi had the decency to blush.

"I told you that in confidence," her blush intensifying.

"And what I can't believe is that you've gone so far as to enroll in school for a job that makes you want to throw up just so you could see the kinky son of a bitch," I countered. "But, here I am, supporting you the whole way. And I don't say a word unless you ask me to analyze something."

Naomi giggled then, turning her face into the cushions to hide her embarrassment.

"Last shift was terrible, too," she admitted. "It was my first shift back since the concussion, and PD watched me the whole time. He was terrified that I would get run over or something, I guess, because he never took his eyes off me."

"Or, maybe, he finally noticed you," I hoped, my eyes going to the road as I watched yet another truck pull into Drew's driveway.

This time a man didn't step out, but a woman.

"Shit," I whispered softly. "Do you think that's the ex-wife?"

Naomi and I watched as the woman got out of the car and stared at it for a long time before she turned in a huff. She marched up the front porch steps, purpose in her stride, as she hastily made her way to the door.

She stopped long enough to pound on the door with one dainty fist before she turned around and surveyed the area.

Her eyes scanned the houses in the neighborhood and stopped on my house.

She narrowed her eyes, then started stomping down the steps once again and heading straight for my house.

"Oh, shit," Naomi scrambled. "Do you think she's coming over here?"

"She can't see us, can she?" I asked, looking behind me at the black house then back forward at the woman marching towards us.

"No," Naomi denied. "But why is she coming over here?"

I studied the woman.

She was cute. She looked almost like me, actually.

I wasn't *that* cute, though. Not like the woman hurrying toward me.

She had brown hair that stopped about mid back, blue eyes, and she was around my height as well. If someone saw the two of us together, I wouldn't be surprised if they asked if we were sisters because we looked so similar.

Her sense of style was much better than mine, too.

Where I wore jeans (the same ones I'd had since college, ten years ago) she wore something much nicer. She was wearing black slacks, knee high boots, and a flowy red shirt that made her look like she was going to a party and wanting to impress.

When she hit my yard I really started to freak.

"Maybe she'll slip," Naomi said hopefully.

The woman didn't slip.

In fact, her badass boots found traction in the snow, making it almost elegant to watch as she hurried up the steep hill to my front door.

"The least she could've done was use my steps," I muttered as she walked beside the walk, marring the beautiful blanket of snow I had in my yard with her stupid boot prints.

She made it to the door and knocked, causing both of us to freeze.

She waited for thirty seconds before she knocked again, this time with her fist.

Both of us stayed where we were.

My cat, Urchin, shot past both of us like a missile, scaring the crap out of both of us.

"Jesus," Naomi gasped. "Do you think she heard that?"

"I can hear you in there. Just open the door, you husband stealing bitch!"

My mouth dropped open and I stared at the door in surprise. "Did she just call me a husband stealing bitch?" I asked. "I imagined that, didn't I?"

Naomi slowly shook her head.

I picked up my phone, the one I'd been staring at for two days since Drew had left my bed, and dialed the number he gave me if I 'needed anything' while he was gone.

I'd given mine as well, but where I wasn't calling him because I didn't want to come off as sounding needy, he didn't call me because he was at work.

He'd flat out explained that he didn't get on his phone while at work. He was a firm believer that phones shouldn't be used as much as they were, and I couldn't say I disagreed with him.

Now, though, I called him.

And he answered on the second ring, surprising me.

"Are you okay?" Drew asked immediately.

I nodded, even though he couldn't see me. "Yes, but your wife just called me a husband stealing bitch."

There was a long moment of silence, and then he started to curse. "I'm about five seconds away from my house. Stay put. Don't do anything rash."

I hurried to the door and opened it, then came face-to-face with me…only better dressed.

"Can I help you?" I asked Drew's ex-wife.

"You can keep your hands to yourself," she said. "And stop talking to my husband."

I looked at my hands, then back up at her.

"I don't know what…" I started, but she interrupted me.

"I don't care what you do or don't do…with yourself. You just need to keep your filthy hands on your side of the road and stay away from my man," she hissed.

"Mom," a girl's voice came from behind her. "What are you doing?"

"That's what I want to know, too," Drew's voice sent chills down my spine.

His voice didn't sound unsure like the girl's, though. His sounded pissed.

Out of habit, I bit my lip and stared at Drew staring at his ex-wife, a look of contempt written all over his face.

My eyes moved over to his daughter, and I smiled at her, even though her frown would've deterred lesser people.

I, however, had to deal with my younger brother.

If I could handle Jonah's surly attitude, I could handle this girl's.

She had nothing on Jonah.

Thankfully, Jonah wasn't all that bad anymore.

He was actually quite a sweetheart ever since he'd found his calling in life, or so he called it.

He'd joined the Air Force and was a mechanic who worked on the fighter jets.

He also had Downy's love and attention now, which was all he ever wanted, and was one of the reasons he acted out as a teenager.

When Jonah was younger, he did everything he could to get his brother's attention. The moment he got Downy's attention, everything about Jonah changed. He's now a completely different person.

"What are you doing?" The crazy woman asked her ex-husband, and my new…*something*. I wasn't sure what to call him yet.

Crazy bitch, though, had plenty of stuff to call him.

'Asshole' and 'pecker head' being two of the main ones.

She didn't look so refined when she was calling him that.

"Umm," I broke into the woman's tirade. "I hate to interrupt your eloquent speech, but you're being quite loud, and there's a yard full of men over there listening. Not to mention your daughter really doesn't need to be subjected to that kind of language."

The woman snapped her head around like a weird alien like creature and hissed at me.

"Did I ask you for your opinion, homewrecker?" She growled.

I blinked, looking from her to Drew and back.

"Did I miss something, Drew?" I asked. "Did you forget to tell me you were still married?"

"Yes, he did," the woman said, answering for Drew before he could even open his mouth. "Our divorce isn't finalized, yet. They're not recommending mediation."

My mouth dropped open, and I looked at Drew.

When he didn't answer, I started to get a really bad feeling.

Was I a homewrecker?

"Drew?" I asked.

He finally looked at me, and the worry I saw in his eyes made that bad feeling balloon into a full panic.

"You're still married."

He shrugged.

"Not really," he said. "We'd have been divorced months ago if she didn't keep dragging her heels."

Well that definitely wasn't the answer I'd been hoping for. Not at all, in fact.

Fucking perfect.

"Alrighty, then," I said. "I'll see y'all later."

I grabbed Naomi's hand as I turned to head back into the house, stopping when Naomi didn't come with me.

"Naomi?" I whispered at her, tears in my eyes as well as my throat.

That caught Naomi's attention, causing her gaze to snap away from PD, who was staring at her and not the fiasco on my front lawn.

"Shit," she said. "Let's go."

She went with me, finally, smiling timidly over her shoulder at PD before she closed the door.

I went to the bathroom, and that's when the shakes started.

"I slept with a married man!" I wailed.

***

Drew

"That was a bullshit move," I said to Constance. "You fucking know we're not together anymore. You're such a bitch."

"Dad!" Attie said in reproach. "Don't call mom a bitch!"

"How about you come inside, darlin'," I heard at my back.

Tai.

"Okay," I heard my daughter's timid voice say. "Just let me grab my phone out of my car."

"What are you doing here?" I asked my wife once Attie made it into my house.

"I'm here to see why you bought your daughter a brand new truck. Was it because you're trying to butter her up to meet your new bitch?" She spat.

I blinked, then moved so fast Constance didn't even have a chance to move back before I was practically on top of her.

"You need to shut your fuckin' mouth," I growled. "And for once in your life think about anyone but yourself."

She narrowed her eyes.

"Think about someone but myself?" She screeched. "I've been thinking about nothing but you for our whole damn marriage! I finally *am* thinking about me, and now you're going to fault me for it?"

"Yes," I said. "You were thinking about yourself when you told me day in and day out how much you hated my job. Or how about when you told your dad how unhappy you were, causing him then to come to my work and ream me out for *working*."

She gritted her teeth. "I love you. I still love you, even though you chose that job over me. I'm willing to take you back."

"The problem there, is," I started. "That. I. Don't. Want. You. *Back*."

I said it with exaggerated slowness, causing her eyes to widen at my declaration.

"You don't mean that," she gasped.

I was nodding before she even finished her sentence.

"And now I found someone," I started.

"That looks very similar to me. Now, tell me again that you don't want me back," she said shakily.

I shook my head.

"I don't miss you. Not even a little bit," I informed her. "I was with her for less than two minutes, and she's the only thing I can think about all day long. I don't go more than an hour before I'm thinking about her. You need to back off. You need to sign the papers. I've given you the house. You've pulled Attie to your side. You've taken the dog. What more do you want from me?"

"You!" She screamed. "I want you!"

"Well, you can no longer have me. I'm not yours. I'm mine," I growled, turning my back on her.

"I'm selling that truck. She has no need for one so new," Constance said to my back.

I turned around and leveled her with my stare.

"No," I growled. "You won't."

"And how exactly are you going to stop me?" She hissed.

I gave her a nasty smile.

"Because I'll press charges against you for stealing it."

With that, I walked back over to my house and was about to go in search of my daughter when something caught my eye.

Movement from the house beside mine. The one that Aspen said she'd yet to see the people who lived there.

I stared for a long moment, waiting for the movement again, but nothing happened, and my curiosity fled just as fast as it'd appeared.

Especially when my daughter came out of the house and flew into my arms.

"I'm sorry, Daddy," she whispered, hugging me tightly.

I hugged her back, bringing her into my arms and lifting her up off her feet.

"Just leave it, Sweetie," I said gruffly. "We'll work it out. We always do."

Attie laughed.

"That's what you think. She's on a tirade."

I looked up as the truck I'd bought for Attie peeled out of the driveway and gritted my teeth.

"When you get back home, I want you to take the keys away from your mother and don't give them back. When you turn sixteen on Friday, that car is yours and yours only, or I'll take it back. Understand?" I asked.

She nodded.

"But what if she takes it without asking?" She challenged.

"Then you tell me, and I'll take care of it."

She sighed.

"Yes, Dad."

I put my arm around her and started walking inside, trying hard not to turn around and head back to Aspen's.

I'd go later after I dropped Attie back off after the get together we were having with the rest of the men on the A shift.

Then I'd set her straight.

I just hoped that she'd listen.

CHAPTER 10

Pizza Slut
-T-shirt

Aspen

Friday - Thirteen hours later

I slammed my fingers down on the keyboard, insanely annoyed that I now had to tell how fun the product was, despite the fact that the person I'd had the fun with was a douche bag.

A knock sounded at my door, and I turned to glare at it.

"Who is it?" I yelled.

"You know damn well who it is. It's the same person that's been knocking at your door for the last twelve hours," Drew growled.

I shrugged.

"Go away," I ordered him.

I could hear him sigh through the door.

"In my eyes, the marriage Constance and I had is over," he started.

I picked up the nearest thing to me, which happened to be a half finished water bottle, and then launched it at the door.

"Go away!"

He left, but not without one last parting comment.

"I still have a few things left in that box that I want to try on you. When you're ready, let me know."

I glared at the box he'd just spoken about and went back to my review.

If you're looking to add a little shock and awe to your sexual repertoire to do with your significant other, the 50 Shades of Grey Greedy Girl G-Spot Rabbit Vibrator totally lives up to the buzz. With its 12 modes of speed in the shaft and three speeds in bunny stimulator, this rabbit definitely get things hopping. Whether used alone or with your significant other, the various vibrations speeds and pulsation levels will take you on a thrilling ride. A luxury purchase at $100, this is definitely an investment in your pleasure, and it's worth every fucking penny.

On a side note, the vibrator is not very proficient. It offers about two hours of battery life before they need replacing.

Not that I used it for two hours or anything.

Oh, who am I kidding?

I would've used it longer if I hadn't run out of batteries.

***

Saturday

"Hello?" I answered tiredly.

My bleary eyes opened to stare at the clock.

"What size do you wear?" A man asked.

I opened my eyes and stared out the window of my living room.

Grimacing, I stood up and stretched my arms high above my head.

"Depends on if it stretches or not," I said almost without thinking. "If it does, small. If it doesn't, medium."

"Shoes?" The persistent man asked.

"Six."

"Thanks. Bye."

I glared at the phone, unsurprised that he'd called me in the dead of night.

I wouldn't answer him any other time.

He had to trick me to get me to talk to him.

And I'd give him that. He was persistent, and he'd apologized more than once.

But apologies don't mean shit to me. It's the actions behind those words that are important to me, and the jury was still out as far as I was concerned.

I shut off the lamp on the table beside the couch, then went to move into the hallway when I happened to glance outside.

My window hadn't been open much, but the angle of the blinds with how they came together in the middle of the wall was open just enough, and at just the prefect angle, that I saw it.

Two men.

One black man. One white man.

Both dressed in black.

Both standing close and talking animatedly back and forth.

Then the black man reached his hand up and slapped the white one on the back before he left.

The white man, apparently my neighbor, walked up to the house and opened the door, looking over his shoulder once quickly before closing it securely at his back.

"Weird," I said. "Why would you come out and have a meeting in twenty-degree weather at three in the morning?"

My question wasn't answered, and now that I had my heat back, my electric blanket was calling my name.

I'd make sure to ask Drew tomorrow.

My eyes fell closed on that thought, and it never once occurred to me that I was still mad at the asshole.

Not until the next morning, anyway.

***

Sunday
0400

The blankets slowly slid down off my shoulder, and my eyes started to flutter open.

The pull of sleep, however, had me only rolling over and ignoring the cold air that was now touching my upper body, absently searching for the warmth that eluded me.

I found it again, then dove down underneath, only to be pulled up short by a hand around my ankle.

Instinctively, I kicked out in blind panic, but whomever had my ankle was ready for that and caught my foot before I could get any muscle behind it.

"Settle down," an amused voice growled. "You're going to take the boys out."

"What boys?" I gasped, sitting up in the bed in a daze, staring around the barely lit room in surprise. "What are you doing here?"

"Come on," Drew pulled me into his arms.

Without thinking I gave him my hand and allowed him to pull me free, only for him to freeze.

"Head to the bathroom and get cleaned up," he said.

"What?" I asked in confusion. "Why?"

"Just go," he said. "Hurry."

I went, shuffling into the bathroom, coming to a stop just inside when I saw all the blood.

"What..." then understanding dawned, and a blush covered my face. "Oh, my God!"

I cleaned up quickly, tossing my stained under garments into the trash next to the sink.

Normally, I'd just soak them and use them as future period panties, but I didn't need another thing to embarrass me in front of Drew.

I came out with a towel wrapped around myself ten minutes later, freshly showered, sans my hair, and staring at Drew who was busy putting some new sheets onto my bed.

"Get some warm pants on," he ordered.

He was acting so calm and collected, as if I hadn't just embarrassed the shit out of myself and him.

"Drew..." I started, but I wasn't sure where to begin.

He stopped me before the words came, and held up a hand to me.

"Aspen," he said. "I'm a paramedic. I've seen way more embarrassing things than a woman with her period."

My cat meowed at me as I passed him, and I stopped to give him a love tap that consisted of me shoving him off my clean clothes before walking woodenly into my closet and retrieving some clothes.

Once I was dressed in my warmest pair of leggings that were fur lined, a pair of wool socks I'd stolen from my brother, Jonah, at some point, and my Uggs that only got broken out on period days, I was ready to go.

Somewhere.

In my own house.

But still.

"Ready," I called, waiting for him to explain.

He nodded, then proceeded to pick me up around the waist, toss me like a sack of feed over his shoulder, and stomp out of my room.

Then out of my house.

When he kept going even further, I started to get nervous.

"Put me down!" I screamed at the man that was currently holding me over his shoulder. "I can't! I'll go to jail!"

But when he crossed the line over the road, I stared at the ankle monitor on my leg in horror.

But it didn't go off.

It didn't even turn red. Nothing.

It was still a bright green.

"What...what's going on?" I asked Drew's ass.

"I'm taking you somewhere," he said. "With me. It was something my ex-wife hated doing."

"What is it?" I asked breathlessly.

"You'll see," he evaded. "No questions."

I blinked, then nodded.

But I couldn't help it. He at least had to answer one before I could sit in his truck quietly.

"How...how did you bypass it?" I asked softly.

"My sister came and turned it off for a day," he shrugged.

And that only opened up even more questions.

I was dying to ask them, but the way he looked at me like I should shut my mouth had me doing exactly that.

Shutting up.

But the questions burned in my brain, and by the time we passed over the lake, I was practically bouncing in my seat with the need to ask.

"Okay," he said. "My sister's the lady that put your ankle monitor on."

My mouth dropped open.

"What?" I semi shrieked.

He nodded.

"I asked her to look into it the first day of the storms, a couple weeks ago, to see if she could get it temporarily turned off." He continued. "And I didn't want to tell you that she might be able to if she couldn't, so I waited."

"Your sister's Risa Fairchild?" I asked. "She's a badass."

He turned to me and laughed.

"She is. I taught her everything I know," he teased.

I snorted.

"That's funny," I said. "So how long do I have until it's back on? And why would she do that for me?"

"I didn't have to do much," he murmured, turning his brights on as he started to look around, scanning outside of his window until he spotted a dirt road. "She, as well as her entire office, were very much aware of you and your case, and none of them wanted to put the monitor on you in the first place. The law enforcement community is funny. It seems like they have two types of people. People that are loyal and faithful, and people that aren't."

"And what does that have to do with them?" I asked.

"It means that a lot of them know what it feels like, and they're rooting for you. They didn't want to follow these orders any more than you wanted to take them. But they had no choice. They sure didn't have a problem requesting a day off from the judge. You'll get a day once a week until the ankle monitor comes off."

My mouth dropped open in pure shock.

"She said…she said that rarely ever happens. That I could request it, but that I should probably look into a food delivery service because it wasn't likely that I'd get more than just the one day I requested," I told him.

He tossed me a grin before his eyes went back to the road in front of him.

He stopped when the trees on my side of the road opened up.

Then he turned, and expertly started to back his truck and boat—which I just now noticed— down what I assumed was a boat ramp.

"There're are a lot of people here for it being five in the morning," I observed as I looked around at all the trucks and boats.

Drew didn't reply as he stopped and got out, leaving me in the truck to stare at all the people.

He came around to my side, though, and opened my door, a box in his hands.

"Put these on," he ordered, handing me the box.

I took it and watched as he left, then turned my gaze back down to the box in my hands.

Waders?

What the hell were we doing?

Nevertheless, I put the waders on, *slowly,* seeing as they were so freakin' tight that I could barely get my leg down into them.

I'd just managed to get the material up and over my shoulder to hook up the Velcro on the front when a man appeared in front of me.

"Uhhh," I muttered. "Hey."

The man smiled.

PD sure was a handsome devil.

I'd seen pictures on Naomi's Facebook page, as well as her phone.

She was a stalker like that.

"You forgot to put your jacket on," he said, pointing to the jacket that'd been in the box, too.

I wasn't sure that the jacket had come with it, but it'd been shoved none too gently in there.

"What?" I asked.

He smiled.

"You need to put your jacket on, and then pull your waders over the top of it in case you have water that gets up over your waist. Then you won't get your jacket wet." He indicated his own jacket and waders.

I took him in, then looked at my body.

The waders looked like they were painted on already. If I added the jacket, there was no way in hell I'd be able to get them up and over it.

"I don't think they'd fit," I said, indicating the tightness of my clothes already. "And what are we doing?"

PD just grinned and walked away, going to the back of the boat where he then proceeded to help put bag after bag into the boat, followed by chairs.

I pulled the jacket on over my waders, knowing it would be impossible to make happen, and walked to the back of the truck, stopping where the boat attached to the truck.

"Ummm," I said, then screeched in surprise when a wet nose touched my cheek at eye level. "Ack!"

I ducked down and turned, coming eye to eye with a black dog that was wagging his tail excitedly.

"Thief," Drew said, also giving a hand signal. "Sit."

The dog sat before the command came all the way out of Drew's mouth.

"Stay," Drew ordered, then turned to me. "Your jacket needs to go inside your waders."

I looked down my body at my chest again, then shook my head.

"It ain't gonna happen," I told him sweetly.

He tossed me a look, then hopped over the tongue of the trailer to stop in front of me.

With deft movements, he ripped my jacket off and tossed it to PD. PD caught it and laughed as I had my waders yanked all the way down my legs by the annoying man. Then he put my jacket back on, zipping it all the way up to my nose.

"Hold this," he said, pushing my hands down at my sides.

I held them down straight as he pulled my waders up and over my arms, securing them all the way before he told me to remove my arms.

"Feel okay?" He asked.

I nodded.

"I can't feel my toes, though," I licked my lips. "And I might have to pee."

He looked at me like I was kidding, then when I didn't laugh, he sighed.

"Hurry and go," he pointed to a spot beyond the trees.

"Do you have any toilet paper?" I asked.

He shook his head.

"Wipes?" I continued hopefully.

He shook his head once again.

"Fast food napkins?" I was persistent.

"I have those!" PD ran to his truck, grabbed a whole stack about ten inches thick, and brought them to me.

I took three, causing him to laugh.

"Thank you," I said softly, hurrying to the spot he told me to go.

I hurriedly pulled my waders down my legs, struggling the entire time to get them where I needed them.

Then, with a little bit of acrobatics, I hunched down and relieved myself, holding the tail ends of the waders that went up and over my shoulders in my teeth just in case.

I shivered, shaking as the cool air met my ass and vagina.

"You done?" Drew's amused voice asked from behind me.

I jumped up, turned, and hastily wiped myself before I pulled my panties up and over my ass.

"Jesus, Drew," I said. "Couldn't you have announced yourself?"

His grin said he clearly didn't care that I was embarrassed, and he walked to me.

"I'm taking that as a yes," he said, pulling my waders back up and over my jacket.

I glared while he did it, but he wasn't the least bit affected by my scowl.

"Ready now?" He tilted his head in question.

I nodded, still unsure about all this.

I was still mad at him…wasn't I?

But it was so easy to forget that he was still married.

He was so nice and attentive.

And I'd slept with a married man! I was such a slut!

But when he grabbed me by the arm and wrapped his large one around me, I instantly forgot about the fact that I was mad at him.

"You'll sit up here," he pointed to a seat that was at the front of the boat.

I started to climb up the boat, but he picked me up around the waist and deposited me where he wanted me, then emphasized the move with a slap on the ass.

I yelped, turning to him and giving him another frown.

"Hey!" I growled, instilling as much venom into my voice as I could.

The annoyance in my voice flowed right over his head, not even affecting him in the slightest.

I glared at him while he got in the boat, then smiled when 'Thief' came up to me and placed his head in my lap.

"Ohhh," I cooed sweetly. "You're just the cutest thing I've ever seen!"

"Don't give him too much love," Drew ordered as he sat in the very back of the boat. "He'll get a big head."

I glared at him, then proceeded to love and hug on Thief all the while PD continued to put the boat into the water.

The massive motor started up, scaring the bejesus out of me, and continued to rumble loudly as we waited for PD to come back from putting the trailer up.

"So can you tell me what we're doing yet?" I asked hopefully.

PD looked at me like I was stupid. Drew looked at me like I was adorable.

So I chose to flip PD off since he was the one giving me the biggest insult.

PD grinned and turned away, his eyes on the nearly black surroundings as we moved.

The only thing that I could see was the area directly in front of me. Two huge spotlights illuminated the lake as we glided noisily through the water.

My soul, despite the crazy circumstances, was happy.

I didn't realize just how bad it'd gotten until Drew had taken me out. Even the truck ride had been excellent.

Now I was getting fresh air that wasn't on my front lawn, and I felt like I could breathe deeper.

I was ecstatic. I didn't care what we did.

***

An hour later I was in hell.

I was freezing. I was sitting hunkered down in the chair, and the two men behind me were having the time of their lives.

I, on the other hand, was not.

That was because we'd hit two trees so far, and one of those trees happened to be dead, making a part of it fall off into the water just a few inches from Drew's head.

He'd laughed about it.

I, however, had not.

I was not in a good mood.

That could've taken his head off. Yet, he didn't seem to care about that…and we were still in the goddamn trees.

And my tits and toes were freezing.

"That was close," Drew said as he flung water off his arm. "That could've hit the motor and we'd have been fucked."

I stared at the trolling motor that'd previously been on the front of the boat, but was now most likely becoming a permanent fixture in the water's depth below us.

Hopefully, the fish would enjoy it.

As well as the light that I could even now see shining at the bottom.

"Ummm," I said. "Did y'all need that trolling motor that just fell off?"

Maybe it was old.

Maybe he didn't need it.

"What?" Drew asked.

I pointed to where the trolling motor had been ripped from the mount it'd previously been sitting on. "It's gone."

Drew looked around me, then cursed.

"What happened to it?" He asked.

I pointed to the water.

"Fuck," Drew said, scrambling to the front of the boat.

"I'd say that's about ten feet or so," PD said with a laugh.

Drew snorted, then reached for the wires that were still connecting the lights to the boat.

He pulled it up, and miraculously it still worked when he put the bar back in place.

"This is a fucking nightmare," Drew growled. "We're never going to get to dry land in time to get the decoys out."

By this point, the illusion was way old, and I might or might not have gotten a little annoyed and pissy.

"Listen," I said. "This is cool that you got me out of my house, but I'm pretty sure that my balls are freezing off."

Both men blinked at me, staring at me as if I'd grown a second head.

"You don't have any balls," PD felt obligated to point out.

"Is that right?" I asked him with a raised eyebrow.

PD shuddered.

"That'd just be so totally wrong," he said, eyeing the skin tight waders. "So wrong."

I smiled.

"So…tell me about you, PD," I said, leaning back in the chair and wrapping the coat that Drew had shed for me back around me. "You know my best friend, Naomi, right?"

I could see PD's eyes narrow in the pre-dawn light, and I had to hide my smile as I breathed in deeply.

The smell of Drew filled my lungs, making my heart start to beat a little faster.

He always smelled like lemon and a faint whiff of smoke.

It wasn't what I would think of when I thought on how a man was supposed to smell, but it was him.

In fact, I was so caught up in the smell that I almost missed PD's answer.

"I'm thirty-seven, and I'm a bit too kinky for your sweet, innocent little friend."

My mouth might, or might not have, dropped open.

Luckily, the darkness that was still clinging to the surroundings as well as Drew's t-shirt blocked my reaction.

"What's that supposed to mean?" I asked. "What, are you into spankings? Like with floggers? Oh!" I said excitedly once my mouth finally came unstuck from my chest, leaning forward so I could see PD when I said what I had to say next. "Are we talking bondage and toys kinky here or ginger anal plugs?"

He blinked at me, then we hit another tree.

PD didn't catch us this time, and Drew cursed.

"Don't you know how to drive this thing?" I asked him. "I'm pretty sure you're giving us all brain damage."

Okay, so I was still upset with Drew.

I couldn't help it.

He'd been married when we first met. How hard was it to mention that you had a wife that couldn't scrape off? *I would've understood!*

"You know about ginger anal plugs, also known as Figging," PD asked carefully. "How do you know about that?"

"I've read some BDSM erotic romances," I said. "It started with Fifty Shades of Grey, and escalated from there. Now I'm on the racier books. I have nothing to do all day, so I've been reading more than normal. I'm currently reading *Slaves Desired Master*."

"Jesus Christ," Drew muttered. "I can't believe we're talking about this right now."

He stood up and pushed us off, but I didn't miss the huge boner he had going on in his waders.

His weren't all that tight, either, meaning Drew liked the topic of conversation.

What he probably didn't like, though, was the fact that I was having this discussion with his friend rather than him.

I hadn't said a nice thing to him since he'd given me his jacket five minutes out from the boat ramp.

And I was pretty sure he was rethinking bringing me.

My ankle chose that moment to throb when a particularly hard bump against a fallen tree jolted my leg against the dog's cage between my feet.

I hissed, causing both men to look at me in surprise.

"My ankle hurts," I explained to them.

Drew's eyes widened.

"I didn't really give that much thought," he said apologetically. "I can let you use my waders once we get to where I'm wanting to get to. It'll give you a little extra room."

I softened for him.

"I'll be okay," I said. "It's only because I bumped it against the cage."

He nodded, not quite convinced, and started forward again.

Finally, we broke through the trees, and he groaned.

"We're here," he said to PD. "Check the depth."

I handed him the paddle that'd dropped on top of my feet to him.

"Don't get any funny ideas with this," I said to PD.

His eyes lit up with mirth.

"Sorry, darlin'. I only play with the ones that are free," he shot back.

I opened my mouth in affront.

"I'm not taken!" I bellowed loudly.

PD gave me two raised eyebrows that clearly said he didn't believe me.

I didn't believe me, either.

I was Drew's.

Just not right now.

He needed to take care of his problem before I'd let him back in my bed.

Hours later, I was rethinking that promise to myself when Drew carried me into his house from his truck.

I was partially asleep and would've probably forced him to put me down had I been awake.

But I was officially exhausted from being out all day and so snugly and warm.

"I'm going to put you down on my bed for a minute while I go get Thief settled in his kennel." Drew said as he placed me on a bed that felt like clouds.

My eyes closed and stayed closed long enough for the front door to close and then I started to hyperventilate.

I was going to have sex with him again.

I was going to have sex with a married man!

Oh, my God!

I was such a slut!

I furiously dialed Naomi's number, relieved when she answered.

"Hello?" She said, sounding chipper as always.

"Quick!" I said loudly. "I don't know what to do!"

"What?" Naomi sounded nervous now. "What's going on?"

I ran through Drew's nearly empty living room to the front door where I could look outside.

I saw him there, standing in tight Wrangler jeans that molded to his ass like a second skin, and stared.

"I'm going to sleep with Drew again," I informed. "Not today, maybe. But maybe tomorrow. I won't be able to help myself."

"What?" Naomi's voice was high pitched at the best of times, but when she was shrieking, it was even worse. She reminded me of a harpy. "When did this happen? You totally told him to suck your dick yesterday and now this?"

I moaned. "I know."

"Well, what changed?" She asked.

"He held a baby," I cried. "At the boat ramp."

"What are you talking about?" She questioned. "What boat ramp?"

So then I went in to the story of how he'd bailed me out of my improvised jail, how he'd taken me duck hunting, let me blow on his duck call, given me his jacket, and had held me when I was so cold I couldn't feel my toes.

But the icing on the cake was when we'd arrived back at the boat ramp, and a baby was there that'd fallen into the water.

The mother had been freaking out because the child was probably no more than a month old.

She'd hit the water and had sank underneath the dark murky depths while we'd been pulling up in Drew's boat.

Drew had bailed almost before he'd come to a complete stop, and had managed to get the kid even before the mother could bend over in her frantic search to get her child.

He'd then started stripping the clothes off the baby, and had placed the little girl against the screaming mother's chest.

"He told the woman to take her shirt off?" Naomi gasped.

"Yeah!" I confirmed. "And then he'd had PD call 911, even though the baby had been kicking and screaming her discontent."

"Holy crap," she said. "What did PD do?"

"Pretty much the same. Tried to calm the woman down. When the woman still didn't cooperate, Drew had taken his own clothes off, then covered the baby with his dry clothes. Good thing he was wearing his waders," I added as an afterthought.

"That's kind of cool," she said. "I would've loved to be there."

"Then I was in the boat and it started to drift off, so I had to start it on my own and drive it. It was so cool!" I froze when Drew started moving towards me, a handful of crap in his hands. "Shit, I gotta go. He's coming back."

"Have sex with him!" Was the last thing I heard before I hung up and made a mad dash into the room.

I didn't go for the bed, though.

There was no way I'd be able to pull off 'sleeping.'

So I chose to go to the bathroom and take care of some of my girly needs before I came back out.

And ended up going through all his bathroom cabinets. And his pants. And his shower.

My eyes lit on the lube that was sitting on the shower rail at the very top, and I froze, wondering what exactly that was for.

Did he masturbate in the shower with it? Why else would it be there?

I had it in my hand when a voice directly behind me made me jump a foot in the air.

"Eeek!" I said, squeaking.

The bottle dropped onto my toe, but I didn't notice as I turned around and gasped, my hand going to my thundering heart.

"Jesus!" I said. "You scared the crap out of me!" My eyes narrowed. "How'd you get in here, anyway? I locked the door."

"It's broken," he said, pointing at the door handle.

The front of the handle had its cap missing, showing the insides of the door handle, which explained why he'd gotten in.

"You could've knocked," I muttered darkly.

His grin widened and he bent down to pick the bottle of lube up off the floor.

"You were in here for about an hour," he teased. "I started to worry you'd fallen in."

I crossed my arms over my chest.

"I most certainly did not fall in. My ass hangs over the toilet seat on both sides. I'm fairly sure it's physically impossible to 'fall in'," I shot back.

He shrugged and placed the lube back on the shower rail before turning around and leaving the room.

I followed him reluctantly, but he didn't stop when he got into the living room. No, he headed right out the front door.

He kept going until he walked into my house, with a key that I'd never given him.

"Hey!" I said forcefully. "How'd you get a key?"

He put something down on the counter, which I could see from the front door, and I grimaced.

"I told you I wasn't eating a duck," I said. "I still can't believe you thought I'd enjoy duck hunting. You're crazy in your head if you think I'll like that."

He tossed me a look.

"All I ask is that you try it, not that you eat it all. That's it," he promised.

I sighed.

"Fine," I acquiesced. "Just make sure you remember I don't like my food burnt."

I came up to the kitchen counter that was directly across from him and hopped up onto it while I watched him work.

Something dinged on my base unit across the room, and the light that'd stayed green the entire day—yes, I checked multiple times—turned from green to red and back to green again.

"Guess that was cutting it close," I guessed. "What time was I supposed to be back in my house?"

He shrugged. "I don't know. I think they give you twelve hours, but we ran way over that today. We were out about fifteen hours or so. I told my sister we wouldn't be back until nightfall, though. When she's working, that's okay. When she's not, we need to get you back here in twelve hours."

"We?" I asked.

He turned the oven on and then started taking down bowls.

"Flour?"

I pointed to the bottom cabinet.

"Eggs?"

I pointed at the same spot.

"We?" I prompted again.

"Yes, we," he confirmed. "The only way you get to come out is if you're with someone who has agreed to chaperone your excursions. That's me or your brother when I'm working."

I bit my lip.

"My brother's not going to agree to chaperone me so I can go out," I told him. "He doesn't particularly like me and avoids spending time with me."

"That's up to you and him to work out," he said. "But I wouldn't count your brother out just yet. Just…trust me."

I got the feeling he knew something I didn't. But it wouldn't be until the next week that I learned what that was.

And to say I was surprised would be an understatement.

CHAPTER 11

I lost one pound this week. Time to reward myself with a hamburger.
-Aspen's secret thoughts

Drew

"Remember to take your sister out tomorrow," I told Downy.

Downy nodded. "I'm not going to forget, you fucker."

I flipped him off and got into the fire truck.

We'd been on our way to go get something to eat when I saw Downy getting out of his SUV, his K-9 officer at his side.

After giving Mocha a scratch between the ears, I turned my attention to Aspen's wayward brother, who had forgotten about his sister earlier in the day, and I had to call my sister to have her change Aspen's day from today to tomorrow.

"Seriously, man," I said. "If you forget tomorrow, she'll be stuck in that house for another week. My sister can only pull so many strings here."

Downy nodded and turned his back on me without another word, and I jogged to the engine and climbed back into the driver's seat.

"What was that about?" PD asked me.

I sighed.

"Downy and his avoidance of anything to do with his sister," I muttered darkly as I pulled out into traffic.

I made my way into the left lane, which was where we were supposed to drive at all times, and headed to Chili's, the one and only place that was open at this time on a Friday night.

We were in the middle of cooking dinner at the firehouse when we had to abandon it to go out on a call. When we came back five hours later, it was a congealed mess and no one was up to cooking anymore.

So, instead of hitting the grocery store for more food to cook, we were on our way out for dinner.

"He forgot about her?" PD asked incredulously.

I shrugged.

"I don't know for sure," I hesitated. "He got a SWAT call about two hours before he was supposed to pick her up, and it ran into her scheduled time by a couple of hours. Then, when he was done, I think he forgot, but he blew me off when I asked him about it just a minute ago."

"Maybe he was stuck doing paperwork," Tai chimed in from the back seat.

I tossed him a look over my shoulder that clearly said, 'I don't think so.'

Tai grinned.

"My wife wants to meet your woman," Tai mentioned. "She's apparently a legend, you know."

My brows rose.

"Why?" I asked.

"Everyone in town's been talking about the scorned cop's girlfriend who went all Carrie Underwood on his car. When Mia heard you were dating her, she told Masen, and that's all I've been hearing about since," he explained.

Masen was Mia's best friend, and Booth's wife.

The two of them together were twin tornados. Add Aspen into that mix, and I feared for the safety of everyone in this town with the antics I could see them pulling if they, *and we*, weren't careful.

"She still mad at you?" PD asked, his eyes going over to Naomi who'd been sitting quietly the entire time.

"Yeah," I muttered. "Won't even give me the chance to get close to her before she shies away."

My eyes went to Naomi's, who quickly looked away before she could make contact too long.

"That's understandable," PD said. "She didn't know you were married."

"I'm not fucking married," I spat. "I'm fucking divorced. My ex just likes torture me by prolonging the inevitable."

"No," Naomi said quietly from the backseat. "You just reminded her of the very thing that her parents did. If my memory serves me right, she told you that Danny cheated on her. She also told me she told you about her mother and the situation with her father. She doesn't do cheating, and you let her do that without her even knowing it, whether you see yourself as divorced or not."

I blinked, surprised that she'd made sense out of it so easily.

Now that she'd pointed it out, it all made sense.

And Naomi was right.

I *had* done that to her.

Despite the fact that I considered myself divorced, I technically wasn't, and I'd taken her choice in the matter away.

She might've made the same choice regardless of whether I'd given her all the details or not, but the fact that I hadn't given it to her was clearly upsetting her.

I hadn't considered how she might view it

Yes, I'd known she was upset, but now that I looked at it from her point of view…

"Shit," I muttered softly.

"Yep," she confirmed. "If it makes you feel better, I told her to sleep with you again, but she told me she couldn't do it until she was sure you were divorced."

When we pulled up to Chili's, I held back, waiting for everyone to go inside, and then I called my lawyer.

If she wanted me divorced, then I was getting fucking divorced.

She was worth it.

***

The papers were signed a few days later.

It would be official, and I'd spent damn near my whole life savings to make it so.

I felt not one single regret as I signed my name at all the flagged spots, then handed the papers back to my lawyer.

"She's happy with the settlement?" I asked Todd Masterson, my lawyer.

"She's as happy as she's going to get," he corrected. "I wouldn't have given her what you did, either, and I'm willing to bet that she would've settled for a lot less."

I nodded.

"I know," I said. "I was hoping she wouldn't balk this way."

He nodded.

"Well, I would say she was quite happy. She knew it was going to happen, and she was just waiting for you to up the ante, so to speak. And up it you did. By way too much," Todd muttered.

He hadn't been happy about all the money I'd given Constance.

Not that I'd given it to her, per se.

It was all conditional. Something that I likely wouldn't have accomplished if it wasn't for Constance's ignorance, and her haste in signing once she saw all the money I was throwing at her.

She had to spend all the money on living. She couldn't use it to buy clothes or frivolities. She had to use it to pay her bills, or anything that had to do with Attie. She couldn't just spend it wherever the fuck she wanted.

And if she broke the rules, she got it taken away with no chance on getting it back.

It also only stayed in her name for two years before it was transferred to Attie's college fund. Once Attie graduated college, she'd get the rest put into a bank account which she'd get a stipend each and every month.

Although it wasn't much, a measly fifty grand in the grand scheme of things, it was all the money I'd had to my name.

Now the only things I had left that were mine were the clothes in my house, my house, and my truck.

I'd be working for the next twenty years, and would have no chance at retiring any time soon, that was for sure.

But I was free.

And it was oddly sad.

Not that I was divorcing my ex-wife, but that I viewed it as a failure on my part.

I didn't like to fail. Hell, *no one* does.

But somehow knowing that I'd promised to spend my life with that woman, and it had fallen apart somewhere along the way, made me feel a bit sad and a whole lot confused.

Adding to my confusion were my feelings for Aspen. I cared about her, and I wanted to be with her. Hell, I was even willing to do it again and that scared the absolute hell out of me.

If I couldn't make it work the first time, what made me think I could make it work the second?

All of those questions followed me out of the lawyer's office and swirled in my head the entire way home.

I was so lost in those thoughts, I was actually a bit surprised when I pulled into my driveway.

The entire ride home was a blur.

I shut the engine of the truck off and got out, staring up at the house that would be mine for a long time to come.

My phone rang, and I groaned when I saw it was my ex-wife.

"Hello?" I answered tiredly.

"I can't believe you did it. You quit us."

CHAPTER 12

Don't cry because it's over. Smile because I didn't end your miserable existence like I wanted to, bitch.
-Aspen's secret thoughts

Aspen

I took the dildo out of the box and was surprised to see all the other items in there.

"Jesus," Naomi said from the phone I was holding. "Why did they send you more?"

I smiled, even though she couldn't see me.

I was pointing the phone at all the goodies that'd come in the mail.

"There's a shop in Uncertain, Texas called Uncertain Pleasures. They really liked my reviews of their products and wanted me to try a few of their other product lines," I explained. "But they sent half their store."

"What's that one sticking to the window?" She asked. "What's the purpose of the suction cup?"

I heard the door open behind me but didn't bother to stop explaining.

I was mad at Downy, and he was four hours late…for the second day in a row.

I wasn't really seeing the point of doing anything with him this late in the day, either. It was now twelve o'clock PM on one of my ankle monitor free days. I had things to do and he'd promised to take me. It wasn't enough time to get back by five, no matter what I did.

I needed to go to Longview and get a new computer. Mine was acting wonky.

I wasn't sure how long that would take me, either, and I didn't want to be too long.

"Oh, my God." Naomi exclaimed. "What is *that*?"

I looked where the phone was now pointing and smiled.

"That, according to my master list, is the…" I pulled out my sheet of paper. "Monster Marcus nine-inch realistic dildo with balls," I read to her. "And it feels like real skin."

I heard an amused snort behind me that most certainly did not sound like my brother, causing me to whirl around.

"What are you doing here?" I asked my ex, Danny.

"I'm here to see if you've seen the paperwork I left here the week before your…meltdown," he replied sweetly.

Without even thinking about it, I hung up on Naomi and turned to face Danny, not happy in the slightest that he was here.

And that he'd just walked into my house without knocking.

That privilege had been revoked when he'd stuffed his cock into his partner while he was still with me.

"Well…" I said slowly. "I threw out everything of yours that was left here. I'm pretty sure your passport was one of those things, as well as your car tag renewals."

Danny's eyes narrowed. "You stupid bitch," he took a threatening step forward.

I held the dildo up like a sword and pointed it at him.

"Don't you fucking think about it," I ordered him.

He stopped, looking from me to the dildo then back again.

"And you think that's going to stop me?" He asked, slapping the dildo aside before he advanced on me.

I'd never in my life been scared of Danny.

Never once had he shown me anything that I would even consider as abusive tendencies. But, right then, with the look of pure hate in his eyes, I knew he was willing to hit me.

I'd pissed him off, and this had nothing to do with the papers I'd thrown away.

"What are you doing?" I shrieked semi-worriedly.

I say semi, because instead of backing up like I should've been doing, I was advancing and I could see that Danny was pissed.

I didn't have any God-given sense, apparently.

And he was about to take his anger out on me.

His hand advanced and before I could step back, it was resting around my throat. Not tight, but definitely not lightly, either.

My eyes widened, and my breath froze in my lungs.

Never once had I had anyone's hands on my neck.

Not like this.

My hands automatically came up to hold onto Danny's wrist, and I felt the pure strength pulsing through it.

"So, what were you saying, Aspen?" He hissed.

I pushed at his chest, but his hand tightened around my throat, hampering my ability to breathe and triggering my need to fight.

And that's what I did.

I fought him.

My nails dug into his hand while my knee kicked up.

He held onto my neck, but stepped back, leaving my body at an awkward angle as he took me with him.

His other hand came up, the palm flat, to slap me across the face.

He would have, too, had my brother and Drew not come in before he did it.

"Let her go!" Downy roared, his hand automatically coming up, sweeping in a round house punch to Danny's face.

Danny saw it coming, though, and stepped back, placing me in front of the punch.

Luckily, my brother was able to stop himself from hitting me square in the face, but he couldn't stop his fist from making contact completely.

It hit me in the shoulder, knocking me forward and down before I even knew what hit me.

Danny released my throat, causing me to fall.

I was sure that was largely due to the fact that he needed them to defend himself against Downy who was now actively beating the shit out of him.

Drew picked me up off the floor, his eyes scanning my face and neck before he said, "You okay?"

I nodded, my throat working as my heart beat frantically.

He gave one quick nod, then helped me to the kitchen where he sat me on the kitchen counter.

He pulled out a butcher knife from the knife block and said, "Hold this."

I held it, then watched in amusement as he walked carefully around the kitchen island, straight up to Danny who was preoccupied holding off my brother, and promptly pulled him back by the collar of his shirt.

Then, with hilarious ease, he began his own beat-down of Danny while my brother watched with a satisfied smirk on his face.

I bit my lip, wondering if I should intervene…then decided to hell with it.

I reached for the bag of chips that were sitting on the counter next to me, opened them up and started munching away.

My brother and Drew took turns pushing Danny around, and the scene playing out before me reminded me of the saying 'Don't play with your food.'

Not because of the fact that they looked like they were going to eat him or anything, but because they were the predators and Danny was the prey.

And he just didn't know when to shut up!

"I fucked her first," Danny coughed, wiping a stream of blood from his mouth. "How does it feel to know she had my cock in her cunt…her mouth?"

My mouth dropped open.

"I never gave you head!" I yelled loudly, drawing the attention of my brother.

He looked furious, sure.

But the look on Drew's face…that was a sight to behold.

He was in a full rage.

With one look at my face, he leaned forward and whispered something to Danny, causing my ex's face to turn from a red to flat out purple.

"My dick is not vomit inducing!" He cried. "She did *not* say that."

My mouth dropped open.

"You told him that?" I cried. "I told you that in confidence!"

Drew's eyes lit with mirth.

"The man needed to know that his dick made you rather have sex with your dildo instead of him," Drew added. "I can see it's starting to add up."

"My dick is not bad looking!" he fumed.

"Actually," I said. "It is."

Danny's face became mottled with rage.

"Take that back," he hissed.

The front door to my house banged open and I immediately hopped off the counter.

"Get out of my house!" I screamed at the woman.

The woman tossed me a cursory glance, ignored me, and walked straight up to Danny.

"Let him go, or I'll arrest you," she ordered Drew.

Drew laughed at her.

"I'd like to see you try," he said to the woman that I'd caught Danny cheating on me with.

Her hand shot forward, but Drew caught it before she could punch him in the face.

"Darlin'," he drawled. "I know you're a cop…but you're a woman. No matter what you try to do, you're never going to be a man. I have the same training as you…in fact, I have more. I've easily got a hundred pounds and eight inches on you, and your form's all wrong."

He pushed her fist away from him, also knocking her back a few steps in the shove.

She hissed and pulled out her gun, or she would have had Downy not stopped her.

"Ms. Meek," Downy said with authority lacing his tone. "You are off duty. You're in a house that's not yours and you were not invited into it. You assaulted a fire fighter, and to be honest, I don't like you all that much. I suggest you take Danny and get the fuck out of here. I don't think I need to tell you how this will go if you decide to pursue this, right?"

Officer Meek bared her teeth at Downy.

"No," she said. "I don't think you do, Assistant Chief Downy. You've made yourself clear, Sir."

Drew let Danny go, who immediately sagged when Drew was no longer holding him up.

"I don't want to see you here again," Downy snapped.

"Except for when you return Aspen's things," Drew added when the two went to leave.

Danny snarled a curse.

Downy's brows rose.

"You took some belongings that aren't yours, Officer?" Downy asked Danny.

"I didn't..." Danny started to say, but the lady dragon stopped him before he could get much more out.

"We'll return it via a courier tomorrow," she replied hastily, exiting as fast as she could get Danny out of there.

"Well..." I murmured, turning to my brother and Drew. "Are we still on for lunch, at least?"

Downy's eyes narrowed.

"You never told me he took your stuff, Ridley," Downy growled grumpily.

I shrugged, not bothering to correct him on my name.

"You also never come over for me to tell," I added. "And you actively ignore my calls."

"I do not," he argued.

My brows rose.

"I called you last week to wish you happy birthday, and you chose to ignore the call three times," I told him.

His mouth opened to deny it.

"I was at SWAT training…" he lied.

My mouth dropped open.

"You're a lying sack of shit!" I accused him. "Do you not realize that Drew would be attending the same SWAT training that you go to? And he was here. With me."

Downy's eye twitched.

I pushed.

Why I thought this was the time, I would never know, but since he wasn't running away like he usually did, I thought I should press the matter.

"Why do you call me Ridley?" I asked softly.

Downy's eyes flicked to Drew, then back to me.

I flicked my eyes at Drew, and he took the hint.

"Be right back," he muttered. "I'm gonna make sure they're gone."

He disappeared in the next instant, closing the door quietly behind him as he went.

"Well?" I challenged him, crossing my arms over my chest to stare at my stepbrother... who was actually my real brother, only he didn't know it yet.

I didn't expect him to answer.

Not really.

And what he said blew me away.

"Aspen was my father's name, and it hurts to call you by that. It's a constant reminder that you're here and he's not," Downy hissed defensively.

My mouth dropped open.

That was the first time he'd ever told me that. Sure, I'd known his father's name. *My* father's name. Stupidly, I'd thought it was an honor to be named after our father, but apparently I was wrong.

"I..." I said. "I don't know what to say."

Downy shrugged.

"I can't help it. I just hear your name, and I'm reminded of how much I miss him. It's nothing against you...it's just how it is," he hedged.

"Okay then," I said. "Well, that sucks, but at least I know now."

I started backing away, a strange feeling welling up in the back of my throat.

"I gotta use the restroom," I whispered softly, backing up faster now.

Downy started to reach for me, but I stopped him with my next words.

"I want you to leave."

Downy's brows furrowed.

"But what about lunch?" He challenged.

I shook my head.

"I think that's enough for today, thanks."

With that I left, not looking back.

If I had, though, I would've seen the devastation on Downy's face.

Would've seen the instant regret filling his eye and in his entire demeanor.

But right then, I chose instead to focus on myself.

Seemed like a good time to do that.

***

It was hours later when I heard my bedroom door open.

I didn't bother looking over my shoulder.

I knew who it was.

Drew got into the bed with me, curled his big body around mine and settled in deep.

The room was dark except for the glow from the street lights streaming in through my blinds.

The clock next to my bed read nine P.M. Meaning I'd fallen asleep, seeing as I'd come into my room a very long time ago.

I lay there, with Drew's arms wrapped securely around me, thinking.

Thinking about what'd happened that day. About Downy and his inability to ever see me as anything but a reminder of what I was and was not. Then finally about Drew. About how he was in the process of divorcing his wife.

And I just wanted to be someone's first choice.

I wanted to be loved by someone forever, someone who'd never chose anyone else over me.

Danny. Downy. Drew.

Maybe it had something to do with 'D' names. Maybe I should look for a Sam or a Michael. Possibly a Luke.

When Drew's breaths finally evened out indicating he'd fallen to sleep, I inched my way out of his hold, heading to the kitchen.

Maybe some ice cream would be helpful right now.

Blue Bell had finally returned to Texas grocery stores, and not a day went by that I didn't gorge on my favorite ice cream. It'd been a helacious few months without it after they pulled all of their ice cream off the shelves, and I still got kind of panicky when I was close to running out.

I'd just put the first spoonful in my mouth when a sound from outside had me walking out of the kitchen to the window that looked out over my front yard.

I moved the blinds down, hunching over so I could see out, and blinked when I saw the same two men that I'd seen in the same exact spot a week ago.

"What are you two doing?" I whispered, absently spooning up some ice cream and shoving it into my mouth.

I'd just moved my spoon down for a third dip when one of them lifted his hand toward his car, presumably using his keychain to pop the trunk open.

Then movement caught my eye as a young girl came out of Drew's house. The further she moved down the driveway, the more I realized that I knew that form. It was Attie, Drew's daughter.

She was nearly all the way down the driveway when she heard the men talking.

She was shielded by the bushes that ran down the length of Drew's driveway, and the men never saw or heard her.

She stopped and turned, peering over the bushes.

And screamed.

I dropped my spoon and my bowl of ice cream and started running.

The front door was locked, bolted and chained, giving me a very hard time as I tried to get out in my haste to get to Attie.

Once the last lock was undone, I slammed the door open.

It hit the wall with a loud thud, but I barely noticed as I started to run down the middle of my yard, straight for the men that now had Attie by the arm.

"Let her go!" I screamed. "Now! *Drew!*"

I screamed for Drew so loud that my throat throbbed.

"Fuck me!" One of the men cursed as he started to move toward his car.

Attie, though, fought back, *hard*.

So hard, in fact, that I was initially surprised.

I froze beside her, unsure of where to grab her to help or to let her continue on her own. She figured it out without me, but she got herself free and lurched for the car, grabbing something that was inside the trunk and pulling.

I chose that time to rear back and hit the other man that was still there, but he caught my fist so effortlessly that I was momentarily shocked.

He hadn't even been facing me, how the hell had he seen me?

And I wouldn't get into the fact that he was still holding my hand as well as pulling a gun out from under his front jacket.

I heard Drew's shout from somewhere behind me, causing me to turn and stare at him running, shirtless and shoeless, directly to us.

He had a gun in his hand as well, but he wasn't aiming it at anything.

"Freeze, Smith," the man that was holding me ordered. He had his gaze on the man behind the wheel of the car. "Put your hands on the wheel and I won't shoot you."

Everyone froze, except for Drew, who kept coming until he was in reaching distance of not just me, but his daughter as well.

Attie had her arms around something that was bundled in a blanket, her eyes wild and scared as she let her gaze dart around this way and that, looking like her life had just been thrown upside down.

"Fuck you," Smith said, revving the engine.

The distinct '*thump*' of the car being put into reverse rocked through the still night air, and before any of us could even react, the man holding the gun on the one in the car pulled the trigger.

The car started to roll backward, but the man inside of it was too dead to stop it.

The one who'd just shot the other man then turned his gun on Drew.

"I'm a cop, if you shoot me, I'll shoot you, too. Then your kid and your woman will have to bury you," the man said.

He still had a hold of my arm, but his gun was pointing at Drew's chest, and I was too scared to do anything that might upset the perilous balance that the two men had going right then.

"Put it down," Drew ordered. "Let her go."

The man let me go, but he didn't drop the gun like he'd been instructed to.

"I'm not stupid here," the man snarled. "My name is Raphael Luis, and I'm on assignment as a liaison with the FBI. Call whomever you want and confirm it."

Drew hesitated.

"I have my phone, Daddy," Attie whispered. "It's in my back pocket."

"Aspen," Drew barked. "Call your brother. Get confirmation."

I moved around Drew, careful not to obstruct his view of the man or the situation.

I reached Attie's back, and it was then I saw that what she was holding was a human being.

A *live* human being.

One with big, bright, blue eyes and long curly blonde hair.

"Mother fucker," I breathed, my hands freezing on the phone in Attie's jeans.

Drew's angry bark of 'hurry up' had me yanking the phone out Attie's pocket and unlocking it without another thought.

My eyes, though, kept glancing back at the girl.

I'd just dialed the phone and put it to my ear when the first cop car came rolling down the street.

And it was then that I could hear my ankle monitor's beep-beep-beep.

Well, that was helpful!

What wasn't helpful, though, was having three more guns added to the mix.

"Put them down," the officer, one of the two that I didn't want to see right then, barked.

"Hello?" Downy answered, voice alert.

"Umm, you might want to come to my house. I think the Wild West is about to make a reappearance," I said. "And hey, can you vouch for a man for me? He says he's with the FBI, and I don't know who to call besides you to verify he is who he says he is."

"The one across the street from you?" He asked. "Dark hair, green eyes. Beard?"

I blinked, surprised that Downy knew my neighbor.

"Yeah, that's him," I concurred.

"He's with the FBI. Introduced himself to me and Luke a couple of months ago," he said. "I told him about the house across from you that was for rent."

I could hear him shutting doors, as well as his keys jingling.

"That was nice of you to tell me who he was," I growled in annoyance. "Would it really have been that hard to say, 'Oh! Hey! You have a cop living across the street from you.'"

Downy snorted, Raphael's eyes came to me, but no emotion whatsoever showed on his face.

"He's not a cop exactly," Downy hedged. "And I didn't want you to know about him. He's not exactly an upstanding citizen that I want you getting all neighborly with."

"Hmm," I said, giving my nod to Drew, who dropped his gun. "Must be why he's got a gun pointed at Drew's head. Got it. See you soon, bro."

Then I hung up, ignoring the curse that came from Downy's end of the line.

"Put them down!" Officer Meek, my ex's lover, screamed.

Her weapon was pointed at Drew, though, not Raphael.

The other officer had his gun out, but not pointed anywhere.

He was obviously the smart one of the partnership.

"Drew, he says he's with the FBI. Put it away," I said softly.

"You first," Drew said to Raphael.

"Same time," Raphael challenged.

They nodded and both dropped the weapons at the exact same time, but neither one of them was letting their guard down.

"On the ground!" Officer Meek spat.

Raphael turned his glare to the woman.

"Lady," he growled. "I'm getting on the ground over my dead body. I suggest you back the fuck off and stop pointing that gun with two children less than a foot away from me."

"He's with the FBI," I said louder this time so Officer Meek, the whoring adulteress, could hear me.

She ignored me, walking forward so that she now had Raphael in her line of site.

"Show me your hands," she ordered.

Then something happened, so quick that I couldn't even assimilate the move before Officer Meek was down on the ground, her arm behind her back.

"That's why you never come too close to a trained individual. You don't want to give them the opportunity to get their hands on you," Raphael chastised.

It would be inappropriate to laugh, correct?

I did anyway, though.

Discreetly.

I mean, the bitch deserved it.

"Excuse me," the other officer that was now on the scene interrupted. "But there's a man in here crying about his head being blown off. Do you think I should call that in?"

I blinked, surprised.

Firstly, because the man with his head blown off was still alive. Secondly, because the police officer was asking us if he should call it in.

"Of course you should call it in, dim wit," I muttered under my breath. "Yes, I think that's for the best," I said more loudly.

The officer nodded.

"Got it," he picked up the mic on his shoulder and called it in.

"What in the hell are they teaching at your police academy?" Raphael asked, letting Officer Meek, the cheater, go.

She ripped her arm back and stood hastily, backing up several paces.

She no longer had her gun, though.

Raphael had somehow gotten that without me seeing it.

And I wanted to hug him.

Drew might not like that too much, though.

Especially with the way he kept glancing down at my yoga pants and tank top, eyes hot, and not in a good way.

I was momentarily surprised that I didn't need a jacket, and in fact, wasn't even cold.

Then I shook my head.

That was Good 'ol East Texas weather for you, though.

Hot one day, snowing the next.

"Listen," I started. "I…"

That was when my brother showed up, his face mutinous as he stepped out of his city-issued SUV.

He took a quick cursory glance around, then pointed at the house.

"Aspen, go inside," he ordered quietly.

This was one of those times that I knew not to argue.

I could tell by the look on my brother's face, as well as the way he was practically vibrating with anger, that it wouldn't be in my best interest to argue. Not to mention he'd used my real name.

So, like a good little girl, I went inside.

But I watched from the front window.

The child in Attie's arms was taken away from her by the paramedics that showed up, a striking red head and a blonde that looked super cute in their uniforms.

They took the child to their ambulance and shut the doors, leaving moments later with a police escort.

The man in the car was the next to be transferred, this one by two large men, both out of shape and not caring in the least that the man was screaming.

I was fairly sure they sedated him before they'd even gotten him into the back of the ambulance. Mostly because one second I could hear him screaming, and the next I couldn't.

Mostly, though, my eyes stayed on Drew.

He looked…odd.

That was the only way I could explain it.

His eyes were wild, and his body was strung so tight that I was sure he was going to snap at any moment.

And when he said something to his daughter, and she started to argue, he said a few short words to her that had her freezing. Then nodding and complying with whatever he'd said to her.

She walked stiffly to the truck Drew had bought for her, and with a police escort, she was gone, too.

I'd have watched more, but Raphael said something to Drew, which caused him to turn to the window that I was looking out of.

He shook his head at me once, and I guessed that meant that he didn't want me watching out the window, so I sighed and stepped back.

Right into an eight-dollar puddle of melted ice cream

"Damn it all to hell," I grumbled morosely, dropping down on my knees to tip the bowl up while catching as much as the melted goodness as I could. "This was the perfect end to one fucked up night."

CHAPTER 13

I'm not saying I hate you. All I'm saying is that if you were hit by a bus, I'd be the one driving the bus.
-Aspen's secret thoughts

Drew

My body was still vibrating with anger as I stopped at Aspen's front door.

"Listen, Constance," I sighed. "I had nothing to do with what happened today, and I don't know what else you want me to say here."

I tapped my foot with impatience, ready to get off the phone with the woman.

"What I want you to say is that this'll never happen again!" Constance said shrilly. "Or she won't be coming back to your house."

I ground my teeth together and refrained from saying what I really wanted to say.

Instead I went with what I knew wouldn't set her off on another tirade.

"I will ensure you, to the best of my ability, that this will never happen again if I can help it," I promised her, telling the truth.

However, I couldn't promise that Attie would never be in trouble again.

I wasn't psychic, and I couldn't be with her twenty-four hours a day.

I also had no control over fate.

Something which I'd had slammed into my face tonight.

"Fine," Constance said. "Make sure you get to the field by ten in the morning. Her soccer game is at eleven."

I rolled my eyes.

"Yes, Constance."

She sniffed and hung up, and I breathed a sigh of relief.

I'd called to check on Attie, but just like me, she was able to deal with her problems and go to sleep.

I'd always been good at compartmentalizing things and so was Attie.

What I wasn't good at compartmentalizing was my feelings for the woman that I could see through the window.

She was laying on her bed, which was directly in the line of site from the front door I'd just come through.

She hadn't heard me, otherwise she wouldn't still be swinging her hips to the sound of the music that was coming from the speakers next to the TV.

She was up on her knees in the bed, her front plastered to the bed, ass in the air.

Her Kindle was propped up against a pillow, and her arms were resting under her chin, one lone finger out and tapping the screen to turn the pages on it as she read.

I could see the outline of her panties through her tight yoga pants.

They were the type that barely covered the ass cheeks, and in the position she was in, they resembled more of a thong.

I clenched my fists, my mind going back to earlier in the night when I heard her call my name in such desperation that my heart was hammering the moment the words had left her lips.

I'd woken up to find her gone, and the scream had come again, this time even more frightening than the last.

Then I'd barreled out the door, my gun in my hand and my heart in my throat, to find not just my woman in danger, but my daughter as well.

And let's just say the next five minutes, after seeing that, had not been the best of my life.

In fact, I was fairly sure that out of all my experiences, that one was at the top of the list of my life's worst experiences, which included even the night I'd nearly died when I was seventeen.

Then it'd only been me that could die.

What was infinitely worse, though, was seeing two of the most important people in my world on the business end of a gun.

That'd been eye opening to say the least.

"I just had *sexxxxxxx*," Aspen sang loudly. To what song, I didn't know, seeing as I had never listened to that song before. "She let me put my penis..."

She kept singing, snapping me out of my contemplation of life and how short it may be.

I walked up behind her, no longer able to resist those hip movements.

Once I reached her, I stilled her hips with both of my hands on her ass, causing her to freeze in place.

Her head snapped sideways as her hips started to drop, but I held her in place and made eye contact with her, letting her know with only the look in my eyes that I wanted her to stay exactly where she was.

She got the message. Loud and clear.

I took her calmness as acceptance and started to remove her pants, grabbing the waistband and pulling down slowly, exposing her beautiful ass cheeks one slow inch at a time.

She shifted restlessly, causing me to pull them down faster than I intended to.

I smacked her ass.

"Stay still," I ordered her.

I needed to be in control right then.

Badly.

Because if I couldn't control it, if I let myself slip just a little bit, I could hurt her. And I didn't want to hurt her.

I wanted her to scream, but not in pain.

Well, at least not only in pain.

A little bit of pain was inevitable. I wasn't built like most men.

I had a cock that hurt…but I also had enough experience that would make it pleasurable as well.

I'd make Aspen crave that burn…and she'd take everything I had to give and more.

"Okay," came Aspen's whispered reply.

She didn't stop moving her hips, though.

It was more than obvious to me that she was anticipating this.

Especially when I got her panties down around her knees and saw the wetness that was already glistening on the lips of her sex.

"What kind of book were you reading, baby?" I rumbled, leaning forward and letting my nose skim the cheek of her ass as I inhaled deeply.

Her pussy smelled divine, and my cock hardened in my pants.

"I-ummm…." she hesitated. "It's a romance."

"Oh yeah?" I asked. "What kind of romance. Read me the last page you were on."

She shook her head. "I can't."

"Why not?" I asked, letting my tongue snake out and lick her.

She shuddered the instant my tongue touched the lips of her sex, pushing back against my mouth, urging me to do more.

"Still," I urged again, slapping the outside of her thigh with the flat of my hand.

She jumped, gasping, and said, *"Jesus."*

She didn't pull away, though.

Didn't tell me to settle down…which she *should* have done.

No, what she did do, was encourage me.

She urged me on with her moans as she leaned her head further into the pillow, completely burying her face. Her hands gripped the comforter like her life depended on it, telling me without words that she liked what my tongue was doing to her.

I stiffened my tongue, running it from her clit to the entrance of her pussy, then sank it inside of her as deep as I could manage.

Her taste exploded on my tongue, and my cock, which had only been erect before, was now throbbing uncontrollably.

I would've spent a lot longer than a few long minutes getting her ready for me, but then her breath came out in shallow pants, and her voice cracked as she said, "I was reading erotica…and picturing you doing the things to me that were being done to the heroine."

"Oh yeah?" I asked her. "I think I saw some new toys in a box. You want me to grab them?"

I wasn't going to grab them.

This time was going to be fast.

Next time, though, I'd stretch it out.

Show her how good I could make her feel and how many times I could make her come.

"Condoms?" I asked her.

"Top drawer."

I reached forward for the drawer as I undid my belt, followed by the button of my jeans.

Once undone, I let both my pants and underwear fall to the floor where I shoved them, and stepped out of them altogether.

My hand found the condoms, and I ripped one off and quickly tore it open, removing the condom and slicking it down over my cock.

This time the thing fit, and I was grateful.

I planned to do her rough, and I didn't want to have to sit there worrying about whether the condom was coming off or not.

"You get my size, baby?" I questioned her, letting the length of my condom-covered cock work up and down the length of her sex, coating my dick in her juices.

She shook her head.

"Yes, sort of," she groaned. "The owner of the company that sent the box to me sent some more…in the right size this time."

I licked my lips, grasping the length of my cock and slapping it down again on her pussy.

Her entrance gaped open slightly as it seemed to clutch at me, and I smiled.

"You want me inside of you?" I asked her roughly.

She nodded her head, pushing back slightly.

I grasped her hips.

"Aspen," I moaned gruffly.

"Yeah?" She pushed her hips backwards at me, urging me forward.

I let the tip of my cock sink inside her slightly, then said, "I'm divorced," before slamming home.

She screamed as I filled her completely, her head rolling to the side.

I growled at the way she seemed to mold perfectly to my length, then slowly started to plunge and retreat inside of her.

My movements sped until our hips were meeting so loudly that a resounding *smack* filled the still room around us.

Her ass rippled each time my hips met the meat of it, causing my cock to fucking weep as all of my senses were assaulted at once.

Then her pussy started to pulse, her orgasm building, and I felt my balls draw up.

"It doesn't matter how many times I work myself. Jesus, I jacked off before I got into bed with you this morning and I'm already ready to come," I told her through panting breaths.

She moaned, her neck arching.

The Kindle that'd been in her hands when I arrived fell in between the headboard and the bed, landing with a resounding crack against the hardwood floors underneath.

However, neither one of us so much as flinched.

"It's your pussy," I breathed, not sure where I was going with my ramblings anymore.

I was fairly sure my brain was oxygen deprived due to the fact that all of my blood was currently funneling to my cock from other parts of my body.

"It's burning me alive," I growled. "If you're this hot through a condom, I can't imagine what you'd feel like skin-on-skin."

She moaned into the pillow, then abruptly pulled up and off my cock.

I stilled, sitting back on my haunches as I willed my cock not to freak out at the loss of her tight heat.

"Lay down," she urged, pushing my chest.

I fell flat to my back with a hard thump, the headboard of the bed knocking into the wall with the move.

She quickly straddled me, her eyes going down to the condom covering my cock, then up to me before she aligned my cock with her entrance and slowly sank down on my length.

My back arched at the slowness in which she took me, but I didn't try to hurry her.

This was a new angle for her, and it was likely that she felt me a lot deeper this way than she did in any other position.

The other women who tried this position with me all said that they couldn't take all of me. But not Aspen. She took all of me and sat her ass down on my thighs while she did it.

I hissed out a breath, my head pushing into the pillow in an attempt to stay still and in control.

Then her hand slid down my chest, from collarbone to pubic hair.

"You okay?" She asked.

I grunted in reply, not sure I could make my voice come out sounding as strong as I'd want it to sound.

If she only knew what she did to me.

All thoughts completely left my head when she started to move.

My hands moved of their own volition to her ass as I helped her along, up and down, side to side.

She gyrated on my cock, the very tip of it repeatedly kissing the entrance to her womb.

"I'm pretty sure I can die a happy man now," I mentioned on a grunt. "Jesus, move faster."

She moved faster.

"Slam those hips down, let me hear those ass cheeks slappin' the tops of my thighs," I ordered her.

She followed my urgings, pulling up and then slamming down so hard that the sounds of our lovemaking echoed off the walls.

Her back arched, and the nipples on top of her perky breasts pebbled underneath her clothes.

"Take off your shirt and bra," I ordered her.

She ripped both off without a word, enabling me to see the way her tits bounced with each downward motion.

"Ah, God," I moaned loudly. "I'm gonna come."

Her hand moved down to her clit, and my hands clenched her ass as my release started to work its way to my cock.

My balls drew up, and my abs clenched as I exploded.

The sight of her working herself while riding my cock obliterated any control that I might have thought that I had.

"Uhhhh," I grunted out my release, my hips bucking so hard that I lifted her clear off her knees.

She cried out as well, and it was only once I was back in control of my faculties that I realized it was in release and not surprise at being forced off the bed.

Her head was falling back, her hair brushing the tops of my thighs.

Her hands were braced on my chest, one just under my right pectoral, and the other directly over my heart.

Her breathing was frantic as her pussy clenched rhythmically over the still hard length of my cock.

I bit my lips and watched her come down from her own high, amazed yet again that someone that beautiful would want me.

Something that I told her moments later.

"God," I whispered gruffly. "You're so fucking beautiful."

A knock at the front door had us both turning to see Raphael's back against the open window that was directly in the line of sight from the bed that we were still laying completely naked on top of.

"Shit," Aspen said, rolling off of me in one swift move, unseating herself from my cock and rolling off the bed.

My still semi-erect cock slapped wetly against my belly and I cursed when I saw that, once again, we'd busted a condom.

"Jesus Christ," I said. "What are the fucking odds of this?" I asked the ceiling, uncaring that Raphael was at the door.

He couldn't see us, and I guessed it was because he was being respectful rather than pissing us off any more than he'd already done today.

"Shit," Aspen hissed when she saw me take off the remains of the condom.

"If we conceive a child, I'm making that place that keeps sending you these fucking goodie bags pay for the birth."

Her mouth dropped open.

"I'm on the pill!" She yelled.

I blinked.

"You said last week you weren't," I said.

"Well..." she shrugged. "I started it after my period ended."

"It's not effective yet," I informed her.

She cursed and stomped to the bathroom, only just now aware of the come dripping down her leg.

I threw the remains of the second shittiest condom I'd ever seen into the trash, and then grabbed my pants.

Yanking them up over my hips, sans underwear, I closed the bedroom door and walked towards the front door, bare-chested.

When I unlocked it, I didn't bother to invite the man inside, I blocked the doorway with my body and glared at him.

"What?" I asked.

He pointed at Downy who was standing down by his truck, his head in his hands, and I found my first smile of the day.

"He saw, huh?" I asked.

Raphael nodded once.

"She'll be embarrassed as shit," I informed him. "Tell Downy to give us five and knock on the door, okay?"

He nodded and turned, relaying the message.

I left the door open for Raphael to come inside, walking straight to the door of the bedroom and opening it.

"Close the door!" Aspen hissed.

I closed the door, but not because she told me to; I was going to do it anyway.

"Have you seen my shirt?" I asked, glancing around the room.

"It's on the back of the chair," she pointed.

I found it hanging by the collar from the kitchen chair that for some reason was in her bedroom and pulled it on.

"How about my shoes and socks?" I asked.

She pointed to the end of the bed where they were resting nicely and I nodded.

"Thanks," I muttered.

"You're a slob," she said, sitting down on the kitchen chair and reaching down to put her socks on.

She slipped first one foot, then the other, into her socks, then worked the one on with the ankle monitor so the sock rested underneath the monitor instead of being bunched up on the bottom.

"What's he want?" She asked. "To tell us why he didn't go to jail with the other guy—well after he recovers from that gunshot wound to his head?"

"He's undercover. Has been working that case for a long time, and hopefully is still working it if they can keep this whole situation under wraps. Why he's here now, I don't know. I didn't ask," I slipped on my socks and boots in half the time it took her to get on both socks. "Do you want something to drink?"

She shook her head.

"No," she pointed at the bedside table where a glass of what looked to be Kool-Aid was sitting.

"'M'kay," I muttered, opening the door and heading straight to the kitchen.

I pulled out a bottle of water from the fridge and turned to face Raphael.

"What's up?"

CHAPTER 14

I don't know who you are, or what you do. Why? Because I've lost all my phone contacts.
-Aspen to an unidentified number that's most likely her mom, but could possibly be her ex-boss.

Aspen

An hour later

"You're sure that the mother's here?" Raphael asked tersely.

Drew didn't answer him, instead pulling into a driveway that looked like it led into a prison.

"Why does someone have to come through Fort Knox to get to a garage?" I asked. "What do they do that they need this much security?"

My eyes widened when I saw the razor wire at the top of the fence. And was that...*electricity?*

"They're a custom motorcycle shop, but that's not all they do," Drew muttered.

"How do you know?" Raphael asked.

He was sitting in the back seat next to the kid he'd helped save.

The little girl was asleep in a car seat my brother had let us borrow, and her little head was rolled to the side, the straps of the seat the only thing holding her exhausted body up.

Off in the distance, past the shops, I could see houses, and even further beyond that was a larger structure that I couldn't really make out.

"Grew up here. And I'm friends with them," Drew answered. "I train with them to keep my skills sharp."

I saw Raphael glance at Drew quickly before turning his attention back to the front.

"Are they going to let us in anytime soon?" I asked softly.

We'd been sitting there for upwards of five minutes now.

"They have to come down and open it with a thumbprint scanner," Drew murmured, his eyes moving to the flash of movement that came from the left behind the shop.

Then a man wearing jeans and a black t-shirt, grease covering his arms from hands to elbows, sauntered over toward us.

"That's Gabe," Drew said.

The man was sexy.

Very, very sexy.

The closer he got, the more my mouth watered.

I had a good man who I thought was sexy as hell, but I wasn't dead.

Just because I was seeing him, didn't mean I couldn't appreciate the masculine form with the rest of the female population.

And damn did he have a beautiful masculine form!

Gabe met us at the gate, and his eyes immediately locked on the baby in the backseat, his eyes widening slightly.

"You got the kid," Gabe said.

Drew nodded as he got out of the truck, offering his hand to Gabe as soon as the gate was open enough for him to slip through.

"We did. You heard?" he asked.

I listened intently as the two spoke about the day's earlier events.

It was now ten o'clock at night, and I was exhausted.

But I'd been given the chance to get out of my prison by my brother, and I'd taken it like the boon it was.

My brother had acted incredibly weird, and when I'd questioned him about it, he'd mumbled something about window treatments and left without another word.

"Just drive around to the back building," Gabe said. "Jack and Sam are there with the mother."

My eyes zeroed in on Gabe as he tried in vain to keep his voice even.

"What the hell happened?" Drew asked quietly.

"Sam and Max met them at the bus station, but the bus had broken down outside of town with a flat tire. Instead of waiting for the bus to get fixed, the woman started walking to town and the man found her about a mile outside of town. Beat the shit out of her, took the kid," Gabe said softly.

My eyes widened.

"Shit," Drew said. "She leaves one abusive situation and enters another. I'm sure she's frantic."

Gabe nodded and pointed. "Go on."

Drew offered Gabe one of those back slap handshakes and got back into the truck, puttering slowly around all the buildings and houses.

"That man helped you move," I pointed at a blonde-haired man.

Drew's eyes moved over to me.

"You watched us?" He asked.

I nodded.

"What else did I have to do all day?" I asked him.

"Mind your own business?" He suggested.

Drew snorted, as did Raphael from the backseat.

"She didn't watch me move in," Raphael countered softly.

I turned around to look at him.

"That was because you moved in at the dead of night. I saw inside your house today. You don't even have any furniture," I shot back.

Raphael's mouth quirked up into a smile.

"That's James," Drew gestured with his chin, and then slammed on his breaks suddenly, causing us all to curse. "And *that's* his daughter."

The daughter in question streaked across the road, running away with a compound bow in one hand, and a quiver of arrows in the other.

"Janie!" James yelled from the front porch. "Open your damn eyes!"

James waved at Drew, his eyes going to the man in the backseat then back to Drew before nodding and heading inside.

A beautiful woman with wavy brown hair barreled into him, throwing herself into his arms.

James picked her up and twirled her around, then put her unclothed body up against the glass wall of the house.

"How many times do you think I'll see bare female asses that I don't have a shot at having tonight?" Raphael teased.

My face blushed fifty shades of red.

"Did you really have to bring that up, man?" Drew asked as he started forward once again.

He made his way to the big building I'd seen from the front gate. The closer we got, the more I decided that it resembled a modern day castle.

"Nice place," I murmured, looking up at the huge building. "The only thing missing is the moat."

"That's what the electric fence up there is for," Drew murmured as he got out.

I followed suit, but Raphael was last out because he got the little girl out.

"Where's the door?" I asked curiously.

Drew pointed to a door that looked like it was about four feet off the ground.

Okay, maybe it was only two, but it was still awkward as hell.

How do you even open a door like that?

I didn't figure it out, either.

A man with graying brown hair opened the door with its magical handle and stared down at all of us.

"Come in," the man ordered.

His voice was deep and almost as sexy as Drew's. The wedding ring on his finger, though, kept me from admiring him much more than that, however.

Mainly because his finger was swollen like a sausage.

"What happened to your hand?" I couldn't help but ask as I was lifted up by Drew and carried like a sack of potatoes until I breached the doorway.

The man's wary eyes turned to me.

"Don't worry, I went to the hospital," he ignored my question.

"Funny," Drew said as he placed me on my feet again. "I would've thought if you were there to actually see a doctor, they would've cut your ring off your finger, Sam."

I agreed, but chose not to voice my opinion out loud.

The man looked freakin' scary.

His muscles bulged as he led the way down a narrow hallway.

"I didn't say I was visiting a doctor. I had just happened to be at a hospital for some other matter I had to attend to," Sam muttered darkly.

For some reason, I didn't think the visit was friendly.

Raphael followed behind me as I followed behind Drew, who stood shoulder to shoulder with Sam.

I couldn't help but compare the two as we walked, my eyes going to their builds.

Drew was taller than Sam by at least three inches, but they looked incredibly close in age and coloring.

They both had tattoos, Sam more than Drew.

Drew's bulk was heftier in his chest and legs, while Sam carried more muscle in his arms.

Other than that, they could've passed as brothers.

It was eerie, too.

Sam took a left at the back of the hall, then we were yet again heading down another hallway, this one thankfully shorter than the previous.

"Give me a minute, okay?" Sam stopped us. "She doesn't know she was found."

Sam didn't get his minute, though.

The minute Sam pushed through, the little girl woke up with a wail.

The mother, hearing the cry of her child, was barreling out of the room and heading straight for Raphael.

Luckily, Raphael let the baby go without any problems, relinquishing her to her mother as the group watched the woman break down.

She didn't look good, and I started to worry about her strength as the woman's legs trembled.

Before she could fall, though, another man with a scarred face grabbed her arm and led her back into the room, pushing through the crowd to do so.

Sam and Drew backed away, letting the man help her through, and then followed them into the office.

Raphael and I stayed in the hallway, unsure of what to do.

I didn't want to butt into their private reunion, and apparently Raphael didn't either.

"Soooo…" I drawled. "You watch the neighborhood too?"

He nodded.

"Every damn day. But I have video cameras. I don't use the binoculars like you do," he winked.

My mouth dropped open.

"You can see me?" I asked in surprise.

He nodded.

"Wow," I licked my lips. "So…did you see the woman down the block from us has a man that comes to her after her husband leaves for work every morning?"

He nodded. "I also saw the woman across the street from me steal a package from her front porch while it was going on."

My mouth dropped open.

"I must've missed that," I told him. "What about that boy who keeps ding dong ditching everyone on the block?"

Raphael smiled. "I scared the shit out of him the second time he tried to do it to me. He hasn't been back to my house since."

I grinned.

"Funny," I said. "I shot him with my water gun and he hasn't been back since, either."

"I know," he said. "I watched."

I laughed, which got the attention of my man who seemed not to like that I was laughing with someone that wasn't him. He opened the door and glared at Raphael.

"Come in here," he ordered. "The mother went back to a back bedroom."

I sighed and followed him in, coming to a halt just inside the entrance.

"What is this place?" I whispered in awe.

The man with the scar who'd helped the woman in earlier snorted.

"You sound like a kid in a candy store," he muttered. "We help abused women find new identities. Different job. New place. No danger."

I nodded, but still not quite comprehending exactly what they did until the man continued to explain further.

"The women that we help are escaping abusive situations. An abusive husband or boyfriend, their parents. Hell, we've even had a few leaving cults. We bring them here, get them new identities, and then help them get to their new lives."

The man's eyes moved to Raphael who was leaning nonchalantly against the door just inside the room.

"But you know that already, don't you Uniball?" The man said, directing that question to Raphael.

Raphael didn't react to the name. Not physically anyway.

Oh, but you could tell he was pissed.

"Why are you called Uniball?" Janie, the girl we'd almost hit on the way in earlier, asked from the doorway.

Raphael looked down at the girl, then grinned.

"Apparently, people think it's funny to tease about someone being injured," Raphael replied to the girl.

"Janie," scar face snapped. "What are you doing in here? You know better than to come in here."

"I told her to come in here," Sam muttered. "Take this to your mom. I bought it for her birthday."

Janie took the present that Sam somehow produced from his pocket.

It wasn't big, per se, but it wasn't small either.

And it was wrapped in duct tape.

How just like a man to do that.

Janie smiled the sweetest smile I'd ever seen and turned and left just as fast as she'd come.

Except she came back less than five seconds later, stopping in the doorway to stare up at Raphael.

"You have pretty eyes, and I'm sorry that you only have one ball," she said, then quickly turned and left without another word, not aware of the reaction her innocent comment got.

I wasn't sure what to say, but Raphael's laughter had me breathing a sigh of relief.

"At least I didn't call you half-sack," Scar face muttered.

"Does anyone call you scar face, Max?" Raphael asked with deceptive calm. "'Cause, if not, I can definitely take care of that for you. Maybe give you a few matching ones."

I looked over at Raphael to see him with a knife the size of his forearm.

"Alright, Rambo. Scar face," I drawled. "Let's go to our separate corners."

All the men in the room looked at me.

"What?" I asked Drew, who happened to have the largest frown on his face.

"Don't you have any self-preservation?" Drew asked softly. "You're in a room full of some dangerous men. I'm pretty sure any of them could kill you in about fifteen different ways with just their hands. Have some respect."

I laughed in his face.

"There's a difference," I informed him. "If you weren't here, I wouldn't be half as outgoing and would probably still be waiting in the car. You'll protect me, won't you?"

I meant it as a joke, but he obviously took it more seriously than that.

"I'd try, baby. I'd likely get killed, but I sure as fuck would try," he promised, whispering into my ear so only I could hear.

The other men in the room found it humorous, though.

From that moment on, however, I was distracted.

He'd give his life to protect me?

Did that mean I'd do the same?

The longer I thought about it, the more I realized that what had started out as a fun little tryst to pass the time had turned into something much stronger and deeper than anything I'd ever felt before in my life.

What I had with Danny didn't hold a candle to what I felt for Drew.

There was just no comparison.

"So the man that stole the girl…" Sam started. "How'd you get him?"

Raphael's mouth tightened. "I've been working a case for months. A child sex trafficking ring that's taken me through fifteen states and thirty different cities."

"And?" Scar Face barked.

"And," Raphael drawled. "I've been here for a while. Monitoring and regrouping. Using the city as a jumping off point to take me to the next drop when I had a call come in—presumably from someone you contacted the moment the kidnapping happened—telling me to be on the lookout. One of my contacts heard the word that I was searching for a girl, and then hooked me up with Darius who thought I was going to be able to help him unload the girl."

"Darius being the guy you shot in the head?" Scar Face guessed.

Raphael nodded. "The one and the same."

"Why didn't you kill the bastard?" Sam muttered.

"Dead bodies don't talk." Raphael said calmly.

A full body shiver took me over at the coldness that seeped into his voice.

"Well, for once we'll agree on something." Scar Face muttered. "But after what Sam got out of him today, I don't think we'll need to worry about any more kidnapping or sex trafficking coming through the city of Kilgore. Jack uncovered three more men that you'd yet to find, and is currently sending the info we were able to procure to your office as we speak."

Raphael's grin was mutinous.

"Excellent."

I had the feeling that everything was excellent. Just not for the men that ever planned on kidnapping young children ever again.

There was not a single doubt in my mind that these men standing around me would hunt down each and every man that they deemed responsible for the incident, and enjoy doling out punishment.

"You okay?" Drew whispered.

I turned my head to study him. "Never better."

CHAPTER 15

With great power comes great electricity bill.
-Fact of life

Aspen

The days after the 'incident', as I liked to call it, went by much faster than the ones before it.

It'd been roughly three weeks since that night, and things between Drew and me had gone from together to *together*.

There wasn't a moment of the day that we weren't spending together if he wasn't working.

Even if *I* was working, he was there.

He may not be bothering me, but he was still there.

"I need to go do some work for the blog," I whispered. "And I have to try out a pot and a cat toilet thing today."

He continued the path he was keeping, letting his tongue trail up my spine.

He'd just gotten finished licking me until I'd come, with little decorum, might I add.

And now he was getting up to go out and meet PD for breakfast.

Or brunch, seeing as it was now eleven in the morning.

"You're going to be late," I whispered frantically.

If he didn't stop, he wouldn't have the choice of whether to leave or not, he'd be staying and finishing me off before I allowed him to leave.

It didn't matter to Drew that PD was sitting at the restaurant waiting for him…and surprisingly it didn't matter one shit to me either.

"I'm not late. We're meeting just up the road. It takes me five minutes," he bit my ass cheek. "To get there. Five minutes," he bit the other, holding on a little longer this time. "To get dressed. It'll take me less than a minute," he licked, starting with the top of my ass crack and moving up until his body was aligned with mine, his cock at my entrance. "So that gives me roughly fifteen minutes. Plenty of time to do what I want to do next."

I cracked slightly.

"But I'm not dressed," I whispered.

He leaned back quickly, pushed me over onto my back, and was in between my legs in less than a breath.

"I'll be quick. I'll use you and let you go," he teased, licking my jaw.

I gave up.

How could I not?

He had super powers in the ways of seduction. Telling the man the word "no" was nearly impossible.

So I widened my legs, allowing him easier access to what he wanted.

He placed his cock at my entrance, then slowly pushed inside, filling me and stealing my breath away all at once.

"Jesus, you're so tight," he grunted, bringing his hands down to my thighs and pushing them up further.

I moaned when his cock was finally seated all the way inside my pussy, the sheer feeling of rightness making my body relax, something I normally had to work at.

It didn't matter how many times he took me, each and every time Drew first entered me was a struggle at first.

This time was no different.

My eyes opened and his abs flexed as he pulled out.

His cock was shimmering with my wetness, the entire length of him coated.

"God," he growled. "I like it when you get that look on your face."

My eyes went to his.

"What look?" I panted slightly, biting my lip.

"The look that says you want me to put my cock back inside you. The one where you're so hungry for me to fill you that you'd do just about anything to get it there," he rumbled.

A sheen of sweat from his workout slicked his chest, and when he leaned forward, placing the entire length of himself back inside of me, the sweat met the side of my legs.

"You're wet," I whispered.

"So are you," he pushed forward and pulled backwards, the sound of my arousal mingling with the sounds of our lovemaking.

His hands moved down, pulling my legs up and over his shoulders, forcing him to go even deeper than he'd been before.

"Jesus," he hissed. "Every single time it surprises me that you can take me."

I wanted to reply, but his cock had stolen my ability to think coherently enough to form a reply, to concentrate on anything else but the feeling of him inside me.

His head turned so his mouth could run along the inside of my ankle, his lips moving over the ankle monitor like it wasn't even there.

Then, as he usually did when we were in this position, his fingers hooked into the strap that held the monitor in place and held on as he started to really move.

My breasts jiggled with each thrust, and I worried maybe I should hold onto them, but then he took care of that for me, leaning down just enough so he could grab each tip between his fingers and pinch.

As usual, it didn't take long before I was on the verge, something he seemed to always be aware of.

Which explained why he started to slow.

I screamed at him in anger.

"Don't stop!" I bellowed.

He grinned, slowing down so much so that he had to let my breasts go to hold my legs up where he wanted them again.

"What's wrong?" He whispered gruffly, biting his lip as he leaned forward, taking my legs with him.

I found myself smashed into the bed, the tops of my thighs touching the bed on either side of my chest.

His cock moved so slowly that I was finding it hard to breathe.

The anticipation of my orgasm had me holding my breath.

I angled my hips, hoping the move would give me the relief I couldn't quite find, and nearly came out of my skin when the tip of Drew's cock dragged deliciously across the front wall of my pussy.

"Shit," I hissed, my body jumping in reaction.

He growled.

"Put your hips back where you had them," he ordered.

I did as he'd instructed, and shrieked when the next pass had my body convulsing.

My orgasm poured over me, washing over me like a flash flood, something I'd never experienced before.

And Drew had given me many, *many* orgasms before.

In fact, he'd given me the best ones of my life, but this one. This one took the cake, for sure.

I didn't know if it was the way he'd gotten me there and then prolonged it. Or if it was because he'd found the perfect spot from an angle that I'd never felt before.

Regardless, it was something that needed to be forever remembered.

"Christ," Drew groaned, his cock jerking inside of me.

Then the warmth of his release flooded my pussy, and I closed my eyes in pure bliss at the feeling.

I was on birth control now, after not one, but two mishaps.

It'd been a struggle to get birth control when I couldn't go out of the house, but after a note from Drew's sister explaining the situation, they'd prescribed them to me.

After I showed them the negative pregnancy test I'd been forced to take.

"That one felt like it was yanked from my spine," he breathed, letting my legs go one by one, then collapsing on top of me.

I giggled, wrapping my arms around his neck, uncaring of the fact he was getting us both sweaty now.

"You're going to be late," I whispered into his ear.

He mumbled something, then pushed himself off me, leaving me in heap on the bed.

"You're gonna have to wash those sheets," he said on a laugh, eyeing my butt. "Sorry about that."

I lifted a hand in an 'I don't care' gesture, then let it fall back to the bed while he chuckled at my exhilaration.

"Your blog?" He reminded me, drying himself off with a towel and tossing it to me.

It hit my lower half, concealing me from his gaze.

"What about it?" I asked, eyes closed.

He full out laughed then.

"Get up," he said, tickling my foot.

I shrieked, jerking my foot away and rolling out of pure reflex.

"Ack!" I said, getting up onto my knees and scrambling off the bed, knowing damn good and well he'd keep at it until I got up.

Once I was out of bed, he gathered me to him and slanted his mouth down over mine.

"See you later, gator," he rumbled sweetly, punctuating the statement with a small kiss to my forehead.

I leaned up onto my tip toes, kissed his scruffy jaw, and replied.

"After a while, crocodile."

***

I had some nipple clamps in my hand, taking a picture of them with my phone, when my doorbell rang.

Dropping all of my goodies onto the coffee table, I stood up and hurried to the door.

I guess I expected about a million possibilities, but not a single one of them was Drew's ex-wife and his daughter.

"I guess since he's spending so much time with you lately that this is as good of a place as any," Drew's ex said sourly, dropping a very packed bag onto the ground between her feet and mine. "But this shit is no longer mine to deal with. Not after what she just told me. Have a nice life, Attie."

Then, without another word, she left and didn't look back, taking the brand new truck Drew gave to Attie with her.

"Ummm," I said slowly. "Do you want to come in?"

Attie burst out crying, throwing herself at me.

"He's going to kill me!"

An hour later I was sitting on the couch, looking across the room at Attie.

She was asleep on the love seat that was catty corner to the couch I was sitting on.

A big, blue afghan covered her lower half, and her arms were curled around a throw pillow that was hugged tightly to her body.

Every few seconds a little hiccough slipped past her lips, and I was officially not in a good place.

The click of my front door sounded, causing me to look up at the beautiful man coming into the room, a large smile overtaking his face the moment he saw me.

Just when he was about to say something, though, I held up my hand and pointed at the love seat.

His brows lowered in confusion, and I sighed, knowing I might as well get it over with.

Getting up and starting toward him without another word, I prayed Attie would stay sleeping and not interrupt until I told him everything that had happened.

Gesturing for him to back outside, I followed him out and closed the door firmly behind us.

Hopefully, if he heard it from me, he'd get all the yelling out before he got to Attie.

"What's going on?" He asked.

I licked my lips nervously, my finger going to my teeth out of pure uneasiness.

"Drew," I said. "Everyone's alright. She didn't kill anyone. She's not sick. But her mom kicked her out."

"You're shitting me," he said stiffly, his muscles locking the moment I got to the kicked out part.

"No," I breathed. "I'm not. She dropped her off to me about an hour ago, and I got the full explanation from her before she fell asleep."

"Okay," he hesitated, leaning his backside against the porch railing and crossing his legs in front of him. "So give it to me already. The wait is worse than the actual act, I'm sure."

"I wouldn't be so sure about that," I muttered darkly under my breath, turning my back on him as I said it.

"What?" Drew asked.

I turned to him, the whole distance of the porch separated us, and finally said it.

"Your daughter told your ex-wife that she was pregnant, and she kicked her out," I blurted quickly.

Drew blinked at me, then he started laughing.

"The girl was always creative; I'll give her that," he said, a smile on his face. "So Constance blew a gasket, then dropped her off. Why's she over here? She has a key."

I winced.

He thought I was joking.

Oh, *shit*.

"Drew," I started, but he interrupted me, raising his arms to grab a hold of the porch's roof.

The move had his shirt riding up over his belt, exposing the taut expanse of his lower belly.

"She could've just gotten away with telling her that she didn't want to live with her, though. Constance knew it was going to happen eventually."

I bit my lip, knowing this wasn't going to go over easily.

This whole thing was about to blow up in my face, and I was right.

The moment I didn't smile, and he finally caught on to what I was really trying to tell him, his eyes grew intense.

Then he cursed, turned on his heels, and stalked across the street to his house.

He disappeared inside, leaving the door to his house open, and stayed gone for less than a minute when he came back out with a pair of running shorts and a pair of tennis shoes on.

Despite the cold weather, as well as the fact that it was about to rain, he ran.

And all I could do was watch until he disappeared.

CHAPTER 16

I hate it when I plan a conversation out in my head, and the other person doesn't follow the script.
-Aspen's secret thoughts

Drew

I ran as fast as my legs would take me.

I'd been going a solid forty-five minutes, and I had passed my usual stopping place not once, but twice.

I'd legitimately ran out of steam about a mile past, but then I saw my daughter's crying face, and kept going.

A loud roar from an engine had me turning my head slightly, surprised to see a car coming up the wrong side of the road toward me.

But they didn't try to hit me.

They were going too slow and were too far away for that.

But what they did do ended up enraging me.

"Hey, old man!" A boy from the backseat of the truck called obnoxiously. "You look a little hot!"

Then the familiar taste and smell of a fire extinguisher was sprayed at me, covering me in the familiar dust.

"Motherfucker!" I growled once the dust had settled.

I'd at least had the sound mind to close my fucking eyes and mouth, thank God.

Otherwise, I'd be in a different position right now.

I cleared my eyes free of the dusty chemicals with my sweaty palms, then narrowed my eyes at the truck that was hauling ass down the street.

Which meant I didn't see the next truck come up behind me, yet another teenager hanging out of the window, until I was being sprayed once again.

Luckily, this time it was one with compressed water instead of the chemical.

It was no less upsetting, though.

Which was why I was stupid and tried to follow the stupid trucks.

I knew as soon as I rounded the corner that I wouldn't catch them, but that didn't stop me from trying.

I slowed once my legs refused to cooperate, and I doubled over, my hands on my knees, as I breathed in and out heavily.

"Fuck me," I growled, straightening and throwing my hands up over the back of my head.

My fingers crossed, and I glared at the ground under my feet, so fucking pissed off I could barely stand it.

My fingers tightened in my hair and I nearly shouted out my frustration.

I probably would have had I not already looked fucking terrible.

"Drew," the neighbor that lived at the top of my street said when I finally made it back to my road. "It start raining on your run?"

I shook my head.

"No, Dolores," I answered grimly. "Stupid kids thought it'd be funny to spray me with a fire extinguisher."

Dolores' eyes went wide.

"You mean those boys?" She pointed at the car that was at the very end of the block.

Right in front of the house that was directly next to mine.

The one that Aspen said belonged to a couple that had a lot of domestic disputes.

Ideally, I shouldn't have gone over there.

It wouldn't accomplish anything.

Surely, all I would be able to find out about the ones that owned the truck was that they were a couple of teenagers, and wouldn't do it anymore.

But I couldn't help myself.

The closer I got, the more decisive I became until I was standing on their front porch, knocking.

The door opened and the woman who answered it looked at me like I was a lunatic.

"Can I help you?" She sniffed, clearly put out that she had to answer the door in the first place.

"You know the boy who drives that truck?" I asked, pointing to the first truck.

The second one wasn't there, and I could only assume that they'd gone home.

Lucky for them.

Because I was about to rip the kid who drove this truck a new one.

"I'm sorry, but why do you want to know?" She snapped.

I gestured to my body.

"This was from whomever was in the backseat of the truck that decided to spray me with a fire extinguisher," I informed her.

She blinked, clearly taken aback by that answer.

"You're telling me that my son used his truck to spray you with a fire extinguisher?" She repeated.

I nodded.

"Son. Of. A. Bitch," she snarled, letting the door open wide as she turned on her heel and started stomping towards the back bedrooms.

She stomped further down the hall and stood in the middle of the doorway glaring at her son.

"Keith Lucas, you get your sorry, good for nothing ass out here right this minute," the woman bellowed.

The door at the back of the room opened, revealing the kid that'd been driving the first truck earlier.

"What, Mom?" The boy hissed with disdain. "I'm trying to get my fuckin' homework done!"

"Did you spray this man with a fire extinguisher?" She screamed at him.

I took a step back, not wanting to enter into this shit fest that I could see on the horizon, and had in fact gotten to the street when the mother came out the door with a fire extinguisher in her hand.

Then watched with silent humor as the mother took the fire extinguisher and slammed it down into the middle of the boy's windshield.

"Mom!" The boy screeched. "That's my truck!"

"It's my truck! I make payments on it, you little asshole, and if you keep acting like that stupid good for nothin' father of yours, you'll have to find your own fucking truck, as well as your own fuckin' house!" She shouted.

I chose that moment to turn my back on the two, jogging across the street back to where I'd left two of the most important people in my life.

Two women who were currently staring out the window at the commotion with smiles on their face.

"God," I groaned as I walked inside. "Don't turn into Aspen," I said to my daughter. "Then you'll be calling me in the middle of work like she does and telling me about the woman cheating on the man two doors down."

Attie's eyes widened. "You what?"

Her eyes turned to Aspen.

Aspen was nodding emphatically. "For real. She cheats on her husband every time he leaves for work!"

I sighed and walked to the bathroom, took a quick shower, and contemplated what I was going to do next.

By the time I got back into the living room and found the two of them on the couch with a box of pizza in between them both, I had some semblance of control.

Taking a slice from the other box on the coffee table, I sat on the love seat and faced my daughter.

"I'm not mad," I told her softly, studying the jalapenos on the slice. "But I'm a little bit disappointed."

In my peripheral vision I saw Attie look down at her lap.

"I don't know even how it happened. I was safe. We were safe!" She urged emphatically.

I laughed.

"Well, honey. Turns out condoms aren't as effective as you'd like to think they are," I said, looking over at Aspen whose face was now a shade of red I'd never seen on her before. "Maybe next time you'll be a little more careful."

She wrinkled her nose at me, but said nothing.

"There won't be a next time," Attie muttered under hear breath.

And I found I quite liked the sound of that.

Immensely.

Before I could go into much more detail with Attie, my pager went, causing me to curse.

"*Shit*," I growled. "I gotta go," I said without even looking at the readout.

I only got paged when I was needed, and apparently, I was needed.

Aspen came up to me and placed her lips against my jaw.

"Be safe," she whispered.

I smiled down at her, dropped a kiss on her lips, then walked to my daughter.

My daughter was watching the two of us with an enraptured gaze, her eyes on the both of us as they bounced back and forth.

Once I reached Attie, I dropped a kiss on her head, then dropped down onto my haunches so I could look into her eyes.

"You need to think long and hard about this, baby," I urged. "A baby at sixteen would be really tough. Although I'm not telling you to do anything rash, I want you to figure out where your head is at when I come talk to you, okay?"

She nodded.

"I'll think about it all, Daddy. I know this is a huge decision," she promised.

"And you can talk to Aspen, too. But you already know that, don't you?"

She nodded, smiling shyly.

"I like her, Daddy," she whispered.

I smiled.

"I like her, too, baby," I whispered back conspiratorially.

***

"Whoa, Rambo. Take a chill pill."

I looked over at Tai, shooting daggers at him from my hunched over position.

"Fuck you."

Tai's eyebrows went up.

"What's your malfunction?" He asked.

"Why are you even here. I'm the one who got the page," I grumbled, crossing my arms over my chest and leaning back further in my chair.

"They called me, too. Remember?" He raised a brow. "We already spoke about this when I first got here."

I ignored him, or at least tried to.

Tai was persistent, which was why I fisted my hands in my lap instead of rising to the bait that Tai was dangling in front of me.

"What's wrong with you, D?" Downy asked, his eyes sharp.

I turned my gaze on to him.

"Nothing to do with your sister," I muttered darkly.

Downy's eyebrows rose, but it was Luke who chimed in this time.

"Why would it have to do with his sister?" Luke interrupted. "Are you two dating?"

I sighed, picking my hand up to pinch the bridge of my nose.

I chose to answer, though, because if I didn't, they'd just keep bothering the hell out of me until I did.

"Yes," I said. "Aspen and I are dating."

"Who's Aspen?" Luke asked.

"Downy's sister," I replied in exasperation. "Wasn't that what I just said?"

Luke shrugged.

"I thought her name was Ridley," he explained, his voice trailing off as his focus was caught by the man across the parking spot from where we'd been sitting.

We were waiting for a warrant to be issued, then we'd go serve the warrant and apprehend the suspect as well as do a thorough search of the property.

Well, *they* would.

I'd be there just in case one of them got hurt.

Which was very rare.

Although last time we were out I had to patch up Nico's arm.

He'd scraped his arm on a nail, and I'd gotten to actually use some medical training.

Not that I was complaining. If I wasn't utilized, then that was a good day, and how I wanted it to be.

"Her name is Aspen Ridley; I call her Ridley," Downy explained when it was apparent that I wasn't going to.

I snorted.

"Downy calls her Ridley because he's too chicken shit to call her by her real name. Which, might I add, breaks her heart. She hates that you don't like her," I told him, turning to him to gauge his reaction.

"I do too like her!" He snapped.

I snorted.

"You do?"

He glared.

"What?" He asked, turning away from me. "I do."

"Funny way to show it," I muttered, sitting back and swinging my legs around when I saw Nico running towards us from the courthouse.

"Got it," Nico breathed heavily, scooting into the seat beside me. "Let's roll."

I didn't reply to the question I could see on Downy's face; instead, I chose to stay silent and let him stew in his own thoughts.

But, by the time we arrived at the house that we were executing the warrant for, Downy's thoughts were all about the job he was about to perform.

The doors opened and I half stood, eyes on the ground to avoid the equipment and feet of the other men in the truck with me.

Then I smiled when my eyes caught on the dog at our feet.

"Your dog's eating your shoe," I stared down at Mocha.

Downy cursed and pulled his foot away, but Mocha had still wrought some damage while no one had been paying attention.

"You're such a bitch," Downy growled, picking his foot up so he could examine the damage. "Anyone got some duct tape?"

A roll was produced from someone's bag, and Downy used it to wrap his foot while Nico, then I, got out of the back.

Nico had a smile on his face when he turned to survey the house, one that quickly disappeared when he got his first look at the residence.

"This is going to be bad," he muttered under his breath.

I couldn't help but agree with him.

The entire damn yard was a junkyard. The place was littered with many, many cars.

And boats.

And deer stands.

And RVs.

You name it, it was there, broken down in the man's front yard.

"This is impressive," Luke muttered as he took his first look.

"They should be on an episode of Hoarders," Downy mumbled. "So tired of watching that show with my wife."

I snorted.

"Your sister makes me watch Downton Abbey and old Saved By The Bell episodes," I informed him. "I clearly have it worse off than you."

Downy flipped me off and moved to the front of the truck, Mocha, for once, right on his heels.

That was something that happened when Mocha realized that it was time to work.

But when it wasn't time…let's just say it wasn't pretty.

I would think she was a terrible dog if she didn't do so well while she was on duty.

But the moment she was off, she was tearing stuff up or eating something that didn't belong to her.

Just last week Mocha had eaten the birthday cake that Downy had picked up for his wife, and everyone in a three block radius had heard Downy's bellow of outrage.

Of course, it'd helped that we were outside at the time.

"Okay," Tai broke into my thoughts. "I think we should talk about this."

"Talk about what?" I asked him.

"About the fact that you haven't shared that you were with someone," Tai continued. "Mia would love to meet her. Bring her to the fire station on Sunday."

I thought about that for a moment, and then shrugged.

"I'll ask her," I mumbled.

It wasn't likely that she'd want to go to a fundraiser at the fire station on her day off from house arrest, but I'd offer it to her anyway.

"Alright, boys," Luke cut in, his voice saying that it was time for business to commence. "I have the plans. Let's do this."

I leaned into the side of the truck and watched as the rest of the SWAT team, including me and Tai, gathered around to go over the plan of action.

"Everyone good?" Luke asked a few minutes later.

We all nodded.

"Tai," Luke said. "You're here in case we need you. Drew, you're with us."

My stomach tensed as it always did right before I went in with the team, but this time was different.

I used to think of Attie right before I went inside, but this time, there was another person added to my worries.

If I didn't come home, there'd be two ladies devastated, not just one.

And I found that I kind of liked that.

A lot.

CHAPTER 17

All my life I thought air was free. Then I saw The Lorax and it all finally makes sense. You pay for the air as well as the potato chips when you buy a bag of Lays.
-Aspen's secret thoughts

Aspen

"What's wrong?" Attie asked as I closed the door on the man who'd just served me papers.

"I've been served," I muttered in the same voice that the man had just used on me.

Attie blinked, her eyes going wide.

"Like, you've been sued, papers?" She asked worriedly.

"I don't know," I tried to be calm, taking the papers from the manila envelope and taking a seat at the dining room table so I could spread them out.

My eyes scanned the words of the first page, and the more I read, the more anger that built until I was about ready to scream.

"What..." Attie muttered as she read over my shoulder. "Abandonment? Who did you abandon?"

I gritted my teeth.

"Apparently, my ex thinks that I've abandoned him, and he's suing me for support. When he's the one who left me," I said dryly. "And the court date is in two weeks. On a Tuesday, no less."

"How are you going to get there?" She asked. "You can't leave."

I looked down at where she was indicating: the ankle monitor that was sticking out of my sweat pants.

"I can't," I agreed. "I guess I'll either have to see if they will let me get off for the day. That or I'll have to request a different day from the judge."

She bit her lip, her finger twirling around a lock of hair that'd fallen down from her high ponytail.

"What?" I asked.

She shook her head, causing another piece of hair to fall from her ponytail.

"You look a mess," I said. "Do you want to take a shower or something? Your mascara is dried to your cheeks."

Her horrified gasp had her bringing her hands up to her cheeks in a manner only a vain teenager who cared about her appearance would.

"Does it look bad?" She asked, patting her cheeks.

I shook my head.

"No," I lied.

She smiled, but excused herself to the bathroom to clean her face anyway.

Her horrified scream a few moments later had me chuckling, even though the words I was reading on the papers had me wanting to scream.

"You son of a bitch," I growled, looking at Danny's name. "You fucking suck."

"Who sucks?" Attie asked as she came back long moments later, her hair back up in a tidy ponytail, and her face scrubbed clean of makeup. "What's wrong?"

I pointed at the papers.

"It states that we're common-law married," I growled. "What the fuck?" I looked guiltily over at Attie. "I'm sorry, but my mouth seems to run away with me when I get all hot and bothered."

She snorted and raised her hand in a clearing gesture. "It's fine. I've heard worse from the boys at school."

I smiled at her, then my gaze fell back onto the papers.

"What happened?" She asked. "I heard a little bit about what you did to earn the ankle monitor from my mother while she was talking on the phone to someone about you, but I never heard why you beat the crap out of the cop's car."

I looked over at her.

"You want to know?" I asked.

She nodded.

So I told her everything, going all the way back to the times when I first slept with Danny.

"I didn't like sex very much either," she whispered.

I smiled at her.

"I imagine that you didn't like it because boys don't really know how to use their dicks at your age," I told her. "Likely, he didn't have the skills or the stamina, nor the knowledge, to make it good for you."

Her eyes widened. "So that comes with age?"

I nodded.

"Age, practice and more practice," I amended.

She licked her lips.

"Would you….one day…can we talk about this one day that's not today? One day in the very far future after the baby comes?" She requested.

I nodded.

"As long as you let me take you to get birth control before I do it," I promised.

She grinned.

"If I'd known you were so cool, I'd have come here a long time ago and spoken about this with you," she whispered.

"Spoken about what?" Drew asked as he walked into the room

My eyes immediately fell on the pronounced limp he had going on.

Not to mention he was covered nearly head to toe in ash and smelled like a supercharged bonfire.

"What happened?" I asked in alarm.

He held out his hand.

"I'll tell you after you tell me what she wishes she would've talked to you about," he said, his voice booking no room for argument.

I sighed and picked up the papers.

"My ex is suing me for abandonment," I told him, showing him the papers.

He took them and his eyes scanned the pages.

They got wider and wider as he continued to read.

"They're saying you're married?" He asked incredulously.

I nodded, my stomach turning summersaults at the look of pure anger on his face.

"You're shitting me," he said.

I shook my head again.

"I'm just going to head over to dad's house," Attie murmured softly, standing up and making her way to the door. "Goodnight Daddy."

She went up on her tiptoes to kiss Drew who'd yet to make it into the room any further, but stopped when she couldn't find a clean place to kiss him.

"Uhh," she hesitated.

Drew didn't have the same problem.

He just grabbed her to him and wrapped his arms around her, ensuring that he got a good hug regardless of what it did to the poor kid's clothes.

"I'll be back in a minute," he said to me, opening the door for Attie and walking down the front walk with her.

The rain that was still coming down, for three days straight now, made them disappear from my view moments later.

Closing the door, I threw the papers down on the coffee table, glaring at them for added effect.

I'd deal with that tomorrow.

Right then, though, I walked to the bathroom and started the shower, and warmed it up for my man.

Then, for added affect, I deposited my body in it and got all wet for him.

In two ways.

Leaning against the shower, letting the water spray me down, I let my hands move over my body.

I heard him come through the door, thankful that he had a key, otherwise I'd worry that maybe it wasn't him coming in, but someone else that wasn't supposed to be there.

I would hate for his surprise to be ruined by someone else.

CHAPTER 18

How do I like my eggs? In a cake.
-Text from Aspen to Drew

Drew

My eyes stayed down as the cold water helped wash the soot and ash from my skin, my legs carrying me fast across the distance from my house to Aspen's.

I waved to Raphael who was sitting on his front porch, who waved back, and then pointed to the side where the boy who'd sprayed me with a fire extinguisher stared at me from the front seat of his truck. He had a friend with him, who was looking at the boy like he was insane.

The truck, incidentally, still had a huge crack in the windshield from the extinguisher his mom threw at it.

"You're a fucking douche bag, you know that?" The boy yelled through his open window.

My brows rose, and I paused, turning fully to look at the boy.

"I'm the douchebag?" I asked him. "What about you? I never asked to be sprayed with a fire extinguisher."

The boy lifted his lip in a snarl, then turned the light bar on his truck, trying to blind me.

"You know who I am, right?" I asked.

I was just being sure he knew before he got himself too far into the fire.

He flipped me off. "I don't give a fuck who you are."

I started laughing then.

"Yeah," I said. "You will care when I decide to press charges against you."

He snapped.

"Prove it, motherfucker. You don't got nothin' on me," he said, tossing the door to his truck open, sliding out, and stalking around it to come to a stop in front of me.

My brows rose.

"How old are you?" I asked. "Sixteen? Seventeen? Eighteen?"

He bared his teeth.

"What does it matter to you?" He challenged, the rain drenching his body, revealing the bones of ribs and the lankiness of his body that only a teenager that hadn't grown into his body still had.

"What matters to me is that I know your parents don't give you the discipline that you need. I wouldn't have gone about doing what your mother did the other day, but at least she did something. My kid ever did anything like what you did to me and I would've had her truck. Then she would've been grounded. Not to mention she'd be lucky if she ever saw the light of day again," I growled, crossing my arms over my chest.

The boy's eyes narrowed.

"Who are you to tell me what I do and don't need?" He growled. "You don't know me."

My brows rose.

"You have a brand new truck. You dress in designer clothing. You live in a nice house. You have a light bar, a lift, and tires on your truck that cost a whack. Trust me, I would be the one to know what you were given," I pointed to my own truck that was very similar to his, yet I'd bought it and not my mommy.

Not that my mom wouldn't have bought it for me had I wanted her to. She was always trying to do stuff for me that I could do for myself. Yet, I never took her up on the offer.

This kid, though, struck me as the type of kid that would suck his mommy's titty until he was pried off with a halligan.

The kid bowed up, and I waited for him to throw the first punch, but reason started to leach into his eyes before he took a hasty step back.

My guess was that he finally saw I wasn't in the mood to play.

"You're a fucking loser," he said, turning on his heel and heading for his truck.

I snorted out a laugh when I made my way to Aspen's front porch, turning slightly when I heard the slam of the door meaning that the boy had gone inside, too.

"Hey!" I heard.

I stopped when I reached the porch covering, then turned to find the friend that was in the passenger seat crawling out of the truck, his eyes wide and worried.

"What?" I asked shortly.

He turned his eyes to the door, gauging to make sure that the boy was actually inside, then turned back to me.

"I'm Mace Turner," he said quickly.

"Okay," I drawled, waiting for him to get on with it.

"I'm…I'm a friend of Attie's," he said.

My eyes instantly narrowed.

"How friendly?" I drawled, hands clenching into fists.

"I've been seeing her for a while…at school. We're just friends." He licked his lips. "Well, we were seeing each other. Then she abruptly stopped seeing me about six months ago. She changed."

I blinked, not ready for that response.

"She changed?" I asked.

I nodded.

"Yeah," he nodded. "But that's not what I want to talk to you about."

I gritted my teeth.

"Well then, what was it you wanted to talk about?" I said in exasperation.

He pointed at the door where the boy had disappeared. "That's Ellison. He's not very nice."

My eyes narrowed.

"Then why are you with him?" I asked gratingly.

He pointed at my house.

"Your daughter lives next door to him," he said simply.

I wanted to laugh.

"Okay," I muttered. "Get on with it."

"Ellison's not a good person. If you're not careful, he's going to do something stupid, and you could get hurt in the process," Mace explained quickly, the words seeming to tumble from his lips in his haste to say them.

"I don't think that really matters at this juncture. He's a kid. I'm an adult. There won't be any more contact between the two of us, if I have my say so about it. But thank you for informing me of your concerns," I said simply, surprised by his worry over me.

He nodded quickly, then tossed one look back over his shoulder before he sighed.

"I have to go home. I have to be at work in an hour. He was taking me home when you came out of your house," he explained quickly.

My head hurt.

"How are you getting home?" I asked.

He pointed.

"It's not a far walk. Just down the street and a left. I'm on the corner there," he explained.

I nodded.

"Be careful," I instructed. "And hey," he stopped. "Do me a favor?"

He waited for me to explain.

"What favor?"

"Stay away from that kid, alright?" I told him.

He winced.

"I plan to," he said. "After that…there's no way I'm going to keep hanging with him. He was only a means to an end, anyway."

I laughed, then, and pointed down the road.

"Go home, boy."

He went, taking off in a jog into the still raining night.

I turned to the door and checked the handle.

Locked.

"He's right, you know," Raphael called from his front porch.

"Why?" I asked. "The kid's a nuisance, nothing else."

Raphael shook his head.

"Boy's got a hot temper," he explained. "I've been watching him. The way he acts around his parents. The dad's just like him. The mom the same to some degree. Neither parent really gives a shit when it comes to the kid, but he gets what he wants, meaning he's an entitled little fucker that thinks he should always get what he wants."

I shrugged.

"So," I said. "There's a lot of that out there."

And there was.

That kid was not an exception.

I also didn't really want to think about it right now.

My head was not in the right headspace to deal with the kid's shit.

My daughter was pregnant.

My ex-wife was blaming it on me.

My new girlfriend was married.

And that wasn't even mentioning the fuck-tastic day I'd had, ending with fucking explosions.

This was a clusterfuck of mass proportions.

No, definitely not in the best of headspaces, that was for sure.

"I'll keep that in mind," when Raphael still didn't say anything.

Raphael shrugged.

"Night," I muttered.

Raphael gave me a chin lift, then got up and went inside, leaving me alone with my thoughts once again, and what I was thinking really wasn't good.

In fact, I would consider myself not very good company at the moment.

Did that stop me from using my key and walking into Aspen's house?

Fuck no.

The sound of the shower running was the first thing that caught my attention, followed shortly by the pizza boxes that were still half filled.

I contemplated grabbing a piece, but the air from the ceiling fan wafted the smell of smoke up to my nose, and I sighed.

Turning around to close the blinds, I stripped my clothes off in the entranceway, dropping them into Aspen's laundry room on the way past.

I could hear the shower running, and my body itched to be clean, so faster than I would've normally gone, I walked into the bathroom, and froze solid at the sight before me.

It occurred to me that Aspen would be in the shower.

What didn't occur to me was that she'd be using the dildo we'd made of my cock.

She had it in her mouth, and while I watched, she took it out, let it trail down her wet body, and found her sweet heat in the next breath.

My mouth dropped open as my dick instantly hardened.

"What..." my voice cracked. Clearing my throat, I tried again. "What are you doing?"

She grinned.

"Warming up your shower," she replied seductively, pushing the glass of her shower door open and revealing herself even more. "Get in."

Her eyes went to my dick, which, by this point, was so hard it was pointing slightly up and to the left. Facing exactly where it wanted to go.

To her.

Grinning and thinking that I had a perfect woman on my hands, I got in.

She stepped back, used some sort of suction cup device from the side of the shower to attach the dildo to the wall, then picked up the soap.

"You're a dirty boy," she whispered, her hands reaching out for me.

I stepped into her, my body shaking slightly as the warmth started to spread over my body.

Water sluiced down my chest, over my hard cock and down my legs.

Bending my head, I wet it down completely before leaning back and letting Aspen take care of me.

Starting with my hands, she massaged the soap into them, scrubbing them free of the dirt, grime, and *other things* that'd become caked on my hands.

Other things being Downy's blood when the explosion had happened.

An explosion that I was surprised Aspen hadn't asked me about the minute I'd walked in.

"What'd you do?" She asked. "Roll in the dirt?"

"Kind of," I hedged.

If you counted stop, drop, and rolling as rolling in the dirt.

Which, *technically*, I guess it was.

I'd not done it out of enjoyment, but out of necessity. Mainly, my fucking clothes being on fire.

All thoughts of clothes, however, were gone the moment she moved to my chest, then further down to my legs.

She purposefully stayed away from my cock, her mouth hovering just a few inches away as she soaped up my legs, even going as far as to clean between my toes.

"Put me in your mouth," I ordered as my dick strained to get closer to her.

She shook her head, and my hand moved towards her, stopping when it met the dildo that was still suctioned to the tile wall.

Then an idea struck me.

"Suction this down to the tub," I ordered, handing the dildo and its holder to her. "And sit on it."

Her eyes widened as she took my dick's twin.

Then, in silence, she suctioned the fucker to the tub, lifted her hips high and positioned herself over it, then sank down slowly over the top of it.

And that's when I became jealous over an inanimate object.

She looked up at me, her eyes heated as she rose up until the tip of the dildo poised at her entrance, then sank down again.

"Wash the soap off you," she ordered breathlessly, repeating the move.

I reached over her to grab the showerhead, removing it from the holder, and maneuvering it over my body.

The soap suds slid down my body, curling around my balls, and streaming down my legs before washing down the drain.

The entire time I watched as her nipples beaded and her chest flushed as she writhed on the fake cock inside of her.

When I looked up to hang the showerhead back up, she surprised me and bent forward, letting the tip of her tongue play along the seam of my cock.

I cursed and gabbed for the top of the shower, one hand curling around the glass door, and the other clutching the shower caddy that was hanging around the showerhead.

She leaned forward and took the tip of my cock in her mouth, her soft tongue licking the sensitive head.

"You taste salty," she licked her lips, leaning forward and taking me back into her mouth.

I let my hand down and trailed it over her shoulder, fisting my hand into her hair when my fingers met the long, tangled tresses.

She looked up at me as I guided her further.

"Ride the cock, too," I demanded.

Her body lifted, inadvertently taking more of me at the same time.

I leaned my head back, and promptly got a face full of water.

Me choking didn't stop her from taking my cock half way down her throat, though.

And I was glad.

I could get over drowning in the shower.

What I couldn't come back from was if she had stopped.

Not when it felt so fucking good having her lips wrapped around me.

My hands moved her head, further and further down my length each time she withdrew, until finally, her nose touched the curly hair covering my pubic bone.

Causing me to see stars.

I looked down then to see her eyes streaming with tears, and her makeup running down her cheeks, but her face was flushed, and she had her finger thrumming her distended clit as fast as she could make her fingers move.

And I knew she liked it.

Letting her hair go, I ordered her to stand.

She let go of my cock with the utmost reluctance, being sure to get one extra lick before she let my cock fall from her mouth.

I reached behind us and turned the shower off.

Without another word, I stepped out of the shower, held my hand out for her, and pulled her to me the moment her hand touched mine.

Then I picked her up, tossing her over my shoulder, and headed for the bedroom, still dripping wet.

I threw her down on the bed as I reached the edge, then bent over to grab a condom from the drawer.

I slicked it down my length, somewhat happy to see that this condom was one of the lubed and ribbed variety.

"Knees or back?" I questioned her.

Her breasts were heaving as she panted, her eyes locked on me and my cock, as she licked her lips.

"Knees," she whispered, then licked her lips nervously. "I got a new toy today to try."

She pointed to the nightstand, at a box that sat inconspicuously on the smooth wood, and said, "There."

I reached for the box as she flipped over onto her knees, her ass wiggling as I pried open the box's sides.

And my heart started to gallop in my chest; I leaned forward, letting the length of my cock play along the juices that leaked from her sweet pussy, stopping once I reached where I wanted to be.

"Do you think you can handle me?" I asked her, pressing the tip of my cock up against her back entrance.

She shook her head.

"No," she admitted. "But I'm willing to work up to it."

I laughed and redirected the head of my cock to her entrance and slowly slid myself inside, stopping once I'd gone as far as I could go, *for now*.

It'd take time for her to take the entire length of my cock, but I'd get her there.

Then we proceeded to see just how much she could take.

And as it turned out…it was a lot.

"I think about you all day. When I'm on shift, and someone mentions their wife or significant other, all I can think about is you and what you're doing. Which new gadget you're testing out, and whether I'll get to reap the benefits when I finally make it back home to you," I whispered against her hips. "And when I'm with you, and you run your fingers over my chest, all I want to do is bend you over the nearest piece of furniture and bury myself inside of you until I can't tell where I end and you begin."

Her eyes widened comically.

When she would've spoken, I placed my hand over her mouth and said, "Shhhh."

Her mouth closed, but her eyes stayed on mine, not straying an inch from my gaze.

"Today…" I hesitated. "Today when my girl came over, you brought her into your home. Gave her comfort. Calmed me down." I continued, "And when I had to leave, I knew she'd be safe in your hands. And it's not every day a man can find someone that'll care for his daughter. She means the whole world to me, and it's becoming very apparent that you mean the world to me, too."

A tear escaped from her eye, slipping down her cheek, and disappearing into the seam of her lips.

"Every day I wake up beside you, I know that it'll be a good day. I know, that as long as I have you, I'll have something to look forward to. I want you to know that I adore you, Aspen Ridley. You're so fucking beautiful, sometimes my heart aches to look at you. Today, when I told my fellow brothers that you were mine, I felt this huge weight lift off my chest."

"Am I?" She whispered, her voice filled with the sound of tears.

"Are you what?" I asked softly, not following her line of thinking.

"Yours," she said.

I nodded.

"Irrevocably. You'll never not be mine," I promised.

She sniffled.

"I love you, too."

I grinned.

"You didn't let me finish," I chastised her gently. "If you'd only given me the chance, I would've said those words to you."

"Say them now," she ordered.

I grinned, then tilted her face up to mine.

"I love you, Aspen."

She smiled, and I dropped a kiss down to her upturned lips.

"And don't forget it."

Product Review

By Aspen

The suction cup dildo holder works great in the bathtub and can easily handle quite a bit of vigorous activity from a multitude of directions.

I tried it out on numerous surfaces and at various angles to see how much it could take, and I was pleased to find that it held firm to all the different surface materials I tried and it was able to withstand being used in different ways without issue.

It's currently retailing for $15.99, and I recommend it one hundred percent.

The mechanics of it are quite simple, and in a pinch, can be used with just a splash of water to make it stick for however long you'd like it to.

The only drawback I saw is that it doesn't allow for anything bigger than three inches in diameter.

But that's not a major issue considering that standard dildos are less than three inches in diameter and would have no issues attaching to this device.

I absolutely recommend this product for inclusion in any sexually active woman's toy box.

Stay tuned to the blog tomorrow for my review of the anal toys that were sent to me for testing and reviewing purposes by Uncertain Pleasures.

Likes: 8,291. Comments: 512 Shares: 1,911

CHAPTER 19

*I'd rather be eating donuts.
-Sports bottle*

Drew

My eyes opened, and my whole head pounded with each beat of my heart.

My eyes started to drift closed once again, but the sound of Aspen's raised voice had me sitting up in her bed, naked and still extremely tired.

We'd had a long night, and I was *not* complaining.

I'd do it all over again. I just wished she'd learn to sleep past nine in the morning.

"What do you mean?" She asked quickly. "I didn't change my account number!"

Her reply was near hysterics. "I need that money! I did *not* change my account number; I can vouch for that right now."

"*No*. Yes. No. You're shitting me," she hissed. "What are you saying, that you let my fake husband change the account number? How is that even possible?" She hesitated. "No. That is my social security number, and no I don't know how he would have gotten it. That's ridiculous."

I walked out of the bedroom with only a pair of underwear on.

"Ewwww!" Attie called loudly. "Put some pants on, Dad!"

I looked down at my underwear, then sighed and turned to head back to the bedroom, all the while wondering why girls had to be so sensitive.

Grabbing a pair of athletic shorts, the ones I'd worn the day before on my run that were now laundered, I slid them up over my legs and walked back out. Just as clothed now as I'd been thirty seconds before.

"Happy?" I asked her.

She smiled from her position on the couch.

"Yep," she confirmed.

"What are you doing here instead of at school?" I asked her.

She smiled brilliantly.

"Today's a snow day," she pointed at the window with excitement.

I went to the door and groaned when I saw the entire yard, as well as all the other surrounding yards, covered with another layer of snow.

"What the fuck is going on with this fucking state?" I muttered darkly, really not pleased that I would have to work in this shit in about two more hours.

"Some people are saying it's the El Nino effect; according to the weatherman, it's just a winter storm."

Ignoring her, I walked over to where Aspen was bent over the kitchen table, her computer in front of her.

She was no longer on the phone, and her head was hung like she was contemplating her life…or murder. I wasn't really sure which one at this point.

My guess would be murder.

Lucky for me and Danny she was stuck in the house. *For now.*

"I think it's time to get a lawyer," I murmured from behind her.

She jumped, a glass of some sort in her hands.

"What's that?" I asked, pointing at it.

She got up and started pacing.

"It's a bottle. Water bottle to be specific. The review for this is going on my blog today," she explained, her teeth worrying her lip as she spoke. "And I know I need a lawyer. I just don't know what the hell I'm doing right now."

She sat down on the couch with a thud, the bottle-or whatever it was- falling to the floor in her annoyance.

"Let me take care of it," I said softly, pulling her back up and into my arms.

She blinked, staring at me.

"Okay," she agreed softly. "But, how will you take care of it?"

I grinned.

"Trust."

She blinked.

"Trust?"

I nodded.

"Trust," I confirmed.

She shook her head, stood on her tiptoes, and pressed her lips to my jaw.

"You need to get ready for work. It's bad out, and I don't want you rushing to get there," she whispered.

I nodded. Returned her kiss. Then smacked her ass.

She laughed as she backed up, back pedaling so I couldn't give her any more of that, then turned towards he kitchen.

"I'll make you a bagel to go," she tossed over her shoulder.

I smiled, then turned back to my kid, who was watching me.

"What?" I asked her.

"I'm happy for you, that's all," she informed me softly.

I walked over to the arm of the couch and took a seat.

"You make any decisions?" I asked.

She shrugged.

"I want to keep it."

I nodded, knowing that would be her decision.

"You know what kind of responsibility that is?"

Even though I asked her, I knew she'd have no clue.

No one could know what being a parent would be like until they actually became one.

The good thing, though, was that Attie would have me. She would have Aspen. She would have my parents, who just might flip their lids when they found out. And, ultimately, once Constance came around, she'd have her mother.

She would never, ever be alone.

Not if I was here to have a say in it.

Twenty minutes later, I was out the door, a warm bagel in my hand.

I snarled silently as my feet nearly slipped out from under me, then turned and glared at the two women that were currently laughing their asses off at my expense.

"Not funny, ladies," I called out.

Attie waved and Aspen blew a kiss.

I caught it, like only a man in love would do, and started back down the driveway.

Movement from the yard to the side of mine had me glancing in that direction.

The kid from next door, Ellison, stood in his front yard and stared at me, hate filling his eyes.

I nodded at him, but didn't receive a nod back.

And when his eyes flicked from me to the two pieces of my heart still standing at front door, his eyes turned...odd.

Then he smiled, making a chill race down my spine.

"Morning," he murmured calmly.

I nodded at him, then kept walking.

I got in my truck, and breathed a sigh of relief when the girls went inside.

Ellison, though, didn't.

He stayed where he was, looking at where they had been standing not moments before.

And I made a decision.

Pulling out my phone I sent Aspen a quick text.

Drew: Watch the kid across the street. He's giving me the creeps.

Then I sent another to Raphael, a man that I wouldn't have thought I'd find a friendship with due to the fact that he'd been holding a gun on me only two days before.

Drew: Kid's giving me bad vibes. Will you please keep an eye on him for me?

Raphael: 10-4.

***

Twenty minutes before my shift started at the fire station, I found myself standing in the chief of police's office. I nodded hello to both Luke and

Downy.

"Pretty snazzy quarters you got here," I said, taking a look around at Luke's new office.

Luke rolled his eyes.

"Fucking ostentatious, isn't it?" He asked. "My wife was responsible for this. She thought since I was the new chief, that I needed to have an office that was warm and inviting. Her and my kids spent the damn day here a couple of weeks ago making sure it was 'just perfect'."

My grin fell from my face as I sighed.

"I got a problem."

He nodded. "Didn't think you'd be here if you didn't," he said. "Hit me with your best shot."

So I did, telling him about Aspen.

"I remember hearing all that when she got arrested for police brutality," he spat. "Knew then, just as I know now, that this is a big clusterfuck. What else happened?"

So I told him that, too.

Luke blinked, his eyes going wide.

"One of my men is doing this?" Luke asked, a note of annoyance in his voice.

I nodded, pulling the papers she'd received from my coat pocket and tossing them down on his desk.

They hit with a soft thud, and Luke immediately started to pour through them.

"Wait," Downy said, silent until now. "You're telling me that douche wad is trying to sue my sister?"

I nodded. "He is."

Downy's fists clenched.

It seemed Downy wasn't as immune to his sister's well-being as he tried to make himself seem.

"I'm gonna fucking kill him," he grunted, standing abruptly.

"Sit *down!*" Luke barked.

Downy flipped Luke off and left without another word, causing Luke to sigh.

"You really had to do that with him here?" He asked.

I shrugged. "Someone had to do it. I have my peace officer's license, but I don't work for you. If I'd have done it, it wouldn't have had the same effect as if one of y'all had done it."

"You're going to get him in trouble," Luke muttered, his tired eyes coming to meet mine.

I shrugged.

"You know what?" I said. "I don't think I really give a fuck. It's time someone thinks of Aspen, here, instead of themselves. It's time for Downy to step up to the plate."

Luke snorted.

"He did step up to the plate," he said, standing now too. "She would've gotten five years in prison had it not been for him."

I shrugged, even though that was the first time I'd heard that.

It didn't surprise me, though.

"Good." Was all I could think to say.

He shook his head.

"Anything else?" He wanted to know.

I hesitated, remembering the boy from last night. The same one who'd been staring at me from his front yard this morning.

Remembering the note of promised violence in his eyes, I went ahead and informed him of what happened there, too.

"Fucking kids," I muttered darkly. "This whole fucking thing is a clusterfuck."

Luke nodded.

"I'll do some research. Do you know his last name?" He asked.

I shook my head. "No. Only the first, but I can tell you his address."

Luke tossed me a pile of Post-Its and I quickly jotted the info I did have down.

"Give me the day, and I'll have more information for you later tonight," Luke instructed.

I nodded, but something in the back of my mind was telling me that it wasn't good enough, stuck with me.

And I was right.

Turns out tonight would be too late.

CHAPTER 20

Dear sleep, I love you.
-Coffee Cup

Aspen

"Look at that," Attie said. "Do you think that my dad would…" she stopped when she saw the look on my face.

"He wouldn't let me, would he?" She laughed.

I shook my head.

"No, he wouldn't," I said, scanning names on the internet. "I think I found you a doctor. It's the one I use for my yearly exams and have used since I turned sixteen. My mom doesn't use her, though. She's too 'hip and modern' for her. She also does obstetrics."

Attie's eyes turned squinty.

"What?" I asked.

She shook her head. "Nothing. I just don't like thinking about…it." She hesitated, "When I first found out I was," she swallowed. "Pregnant. I did some research."

I laughed then at the look on her face.

"It's not very pretty," I said. "But it's got a good benefit at the end," I supplied, standing up when I heard the doorbell ring.

She snorted.

"I guess," she grumbled. "I wasn't very happy to find out. The guy I was with…" she looked down at her lap and I paused. I hadn't heard anything about this 'guy.' I'd asked, of course, but she'd been pretty tight lipped about him. "He told me he put on a condom. And he also convinced me to do it in the first place."

I stopped with my hand on the knob.

I didn't bother rushing to answer it. It was the mailman, and he usually just left my belongings on the front porch for me and left without waiting for me to answer.

"You didn't want to do it?" I asked in surprise.

She shook her head.

"I, well, I fell in with a bad crowd. When my parents divorced, I decided to find some other friends since mine thought bringing it up every five minutes would help me get over it." She bit her lip. "And so I found different friends that knew nothing about me…and that's where Ellison came in."

"Ellison," I tested the name. It was familiar. "Why does that name sound so familiar?"

She pointed across the street.

"That's him," she said, pointing to the front yard.

I looked out the side window at the yard directly next to Drew's, and my heart dropped.

"No," I gasped, voice low and unsteady. "You and him?"

She nodded, wincing. "I can't say it was my best moment."

A knock sounded again, and without thinking I opened it and blinked at the young man on my stoop.

"Can I help you?" I asked him.

He was young, maybe Attie's age if not just a year or so older.

He was wearing blue jeans, a black polo shirt, works boots, and a Letterman jacket that declared him a member of the Kilgore Bulldogs.

His hair was cut in a military style, trim and neat.

His eyes were the color of muddy water, and they were completely and totally focused on Attie who was sitting on the couch staring at him in shock with her mouth open.

He was big, too. Oh, boy, was he big.

Bigger than Drew, *big*, and Drew was no slouch in that department.

Drew was six three and two hundred and eleven pounds. I'd seen a weigh in on the scale just this morning.

This boy, though, easily had fifty pounds on him.

And about five inches.

"Hello," I called. "Can I help you?"

The boy's eyes turned down to me, and he smiled.

"I'm Mace Turner," he rumbled quietly. "I'm looking for her."

He pointed at Attie, who squeaked and ran away, slamming the door to the bathroom in her haste.

"I'm not sure she wants to see you," I told him carefully.

He laughed.

"Yeah," he agreed. "She'll want to see me. Just let her fix what she thinks is needing to be fixed. I'll wait out here."

I snorted and gestured to the couch.

"Have a seat, young man," I gestured. "Can I interest you in some water?"

He pointed at the bottle I'd dropped earlier while talking to Drew.

"I have one of those," he says. "Use it during football practice. Works awesome to mix up the protein powder or some PowerAde."

I smiled, picking the bottle up.

"I have to do a review on it," I said, placing it on the counter and walking to the kitchen cabinet.

"I don't think you're supposed to use that kind of stuff in it," Mace said carefully.

I looked down at the Kool-Aid powder in my hand, then promptly stuck my tongue out at him.

"Beggars can't be choosers," I told him, taking the bottle, twisting the top off, then putting the powder into the top where the directions indicated.

Once I filled the bottle up with water, I replaced the lid, then watched as the button on the top depressed on its own, as the water infused with the powder, becoming the perfect consistency without me having to lift a finger.

"Sweet," I hummed, popping the top and taking my first drink.

It tasted perfect, too.

"Works better with actual protein powder," Mace offered his two cents.

I stuck my tongue out at him.

"So…Attie," I started.

Attie chose that moment to come out of the background, and Mace's eyes lit with an inner fire that I often saw in Drew's eyes when he looked at me.

He turned and looked over his shoulder without turning around, and Attie's eyes widened.

"You're…here," she said softly.

Mace nodded.

"Told you I would be."

Attie's return smile was brilliant.

And suddenly I felt like I was intruding.

"I'm just going to take my laptop on the front porch and try to get today's blog post written, okay?" I said softly.

Mace's head turned back toward me, and he nodded once, thankfulness brimming in his eyes.

"You need more clothes on than that," he said. "Wind's got a bite to it."

I snorted and left the room without another word, grabbed the snow boots I'd written a review on last week and shoved my feet into them.

The next thing I grabbed was the huge parka lined with a Sherpa like material that belonged to Drew.

The back read 'KFD' and it not only went all the way to the ground, it also drug behind me like a train when I wore it.

He'd given it to me last night when I told him I wanted to watch the snow and hadn't taken it back this morning when he'd driven to work.

I moaned at the smell that wafted off it when I wrapped it around my shoulders, my eyes nearly crossing when I groaned in pleasure.

It smelled exactly like Drew.

Lemon with a hint of whatever aftershave he used.

I wished that I could bottle the smell and make a candle out of it.

Not to mention the smell turned me on.

Grabbing the laptop that'd been charging all morning in case the power went out, I stepped outside and was immediately assaulted with the cold winter air.

It was a cold twenty-five out, and the snow that was supposed to continue through the afternoon fell steadily in soft, fluffy flakes.

Although I was nice and warm in my coat, I still walked back inside and grabbed the quilt Downy had brought back, freshly laundered, and laid it down over my rocking chair before I took a seat in it.

Then, I wrapped it around my body, and got situated before I got my laptop out and started on my review.

I'd gotten about two lines in when I felt someone's eyes on me.

Looking up, I smiled at Raphael.

"Hey!" I waved.

Raphael nodded, got in his truck, and pulled out of his driveway.

He was about halfway down the street when I felt another presence, causing me to look to the side.

"Don't move," the boy snapped.

Ellison.

He looked cold.

He was wearing nothing but a long sleeved tee, a pair of dark washed jeans, and a pair of lime green Jordan's that would likely get ruined in the snow.

Oh, and he had a gun.

Pointed at my face.

I blinked, my fingers freezing on keys, and looked up from the gun to his eyes.

"What do you want?" I asked carefully, my fingers gripping the computer with a grip that would likely pain me in the morning.

"Get up. Go inside," he gestured to the door with a red can that was in his hand.

My body froze, eyes going wide at the sight of the gas can in his hand.

I couldn't tell you why that made my throat swell and my heart stutter in my chest.

Both the gun and the can of gas were troubling, but the gun was the more imminent threat to have right then; but you wouldn't be able to tell my body that.

"Go!" He screamed.

My eyes went sideways as I rose from my chair, placing the computer on the chair where I'd been sitting and turning to walk inside.

"Don't do anything stupid," Ellison ordered gruffly.

I opened the door to my house.

***

Drew

"Where's your head at?" Tai asked as he shoved his hands into his pockets.

I dropped my phone into my pants pocket and pulled the hood back up over my head.

"That was Raphael, my neighbor. He said he had to leave," I muttered, my stomach suddenly sinking.

I couldn't explain it, but getting that call from Raphael saying he had to leave had my belly somewhere near my knees.

"I need to run by the house and get my parka," I informed him. "I left it at the house last night. Do you think the boys will go for a run to the house?"

"I don't see why not," Tai shrugged. "It's less than five minutes from the station. Technically, we wouldn't even have to leave there if we didn't want to. Plus, I'm sure Chief Allen would let us stay there due to the fact that there's no power at the station."

"The engine and medic would be in the snow, though. I doubt he'd like that very much," I said, playing devil's advocate.

Tai shrugged. "Back the medic into your car port. The engine will be fine."

I nodded and turned to see what the guys' thought, and they were all for it.

Apparently, sitting in a dark station with no electricity was a good motivator.

Five minutes later and we were pulling onto my street.

On the way, we'd decided to use the Morrison house that were at the top of the street as a place to park the engine. The Morrisons went down to Florida every December and January, something I'd found out during one of my many runs through the neighborhood since I'd moved there.

The Morrisons usually parked a massive gooseneck motor home there when they weren't using it, and it was the perfect size for the quint.

It was five houses down from mine, which meant it was about as ideal as it was going to get under the circumstances we were currently dealing with.

"Damn, that's impressive," Booth called.

"What?" I asked, engaging the parking break.

"The fact that you just backed up in less than five seconds, in the snow. With almost zero visibility," Booth indicated the steering wheel. "You're good at it."

I snorted.

"Been doing it for going on twenty years now," I grunted. "I should be."

Booth grinned and popped the door open.

I followed suit and started walking towards the boys that'd taken the ambulance down to my house.

Booth and Tai fell into step beside me as PD and Bowe emerged from the ambulance they backed to the end of my driveway, under the car port.

We were nearly neck and neck when a shot rang out from Aspen's house, having my every nerve ending spark to life.

My legs started carrying me towards the door to Aspen's house before I'd consciously told myself I should.

Instinct kicked in, and I was running blindly towards the door when I was tackled from behind.

"Stop," Booth hissed when I went to push up.

I froze at the pure authority that leached out of his voice, and reason came back to me in a snap.

"Okay," I licked my lips. "Okay."

Booth got off me almost as quickly as he got there, and I pushed up onto my hands and knees, scrambling to the window next to the rest of the men.

"What's going on?" I whispered frantically.

"Young kid with a gun and a can of gas. He's pouring it all over the living room. The couch. Walking back to a bedroom now."

"Motherfucker," I hissed, duck walking away from the living room window, thankful as fuck that Aspen had left it open like she always did.

Once I reached the garage, I rounded the side of her house and made it into her backyard.

We didn't go out there much. The only thing you could really do was walk around the edge of the house due to the hill that doubled as her backyard.

Although it was big, and fenced, it really wasn't something anyone could ever find as functional.

"That door right there leads to the garage, which'll then lead up into the side of the kitchen," I directed PD and Tai.

Tai and PD nodded, disappearing inside.

"I called for backup," Booth spoke from my back.

I'd heard, which was why I hadn't bothered to tell him how to do his job.

He knew it almost better than the rest of us.

I was in the Army for four years, right out of high school, and it just wasn't for me.

Once I had my schooling done, I'd gotten out, then immediately started training to be a firefighter.

Although I did have tactical experience since I'd joined the SWAT team, I wasn't Booth, who had nearly a decade under his belt filled with experience.

So when Booth wanted to take the lead, I let him.

Not because I wanted to, but because I was smart.

My daughter, and the woman that I knew would be sharing my bed for the rest of my days, were in that house with a fucking psycho.

I sure as hell wasn't going to put them into any more danger if I could help it.

"We go in, I want you to get your daughter. She'll trust you more than she'll trust me," he said. "I'll get Aspen."

But it turns out, that Aspen could damn well save herself, which she did, not even twenty seconds after we'd breached the door.

One second we were hurrying through the kitchen, and the next we were stopping in awe as Aspen took some of the chains off the swing she'd been sent to try and review, and had launched them at the boy's face.

The chains hit Ellison's nose with a sickening thump, blood spraying out in an arc as Ellison's head was whipped to the side due to the force of the blow.

Horrified at what she'd done, Aspen immediately threw her hands out as if to catch Ellison, but stopped before she could touch him and let his body fall to the ground.

The gun that'd been in his right hand clattered to the floor beside him, and Aspen immediately dove down and captured it, backing away while she looked over her shoulder at what I could now see was Mace and my daughter.

"Jesus Christ on a cracker," Booth muttered. "That could have made one fuck of a YouTube video."

Aspen's head whipped around, and then her face broke as she started running towards me.

"What are you doing here?" She wailed loudly.

"Obviously not saving you." I muttered under my breath. "I came over to talk to you. And get my coat," I plucked the jacket that was covering her small frame with my fingers. "And found this."

She hiccupped, and I wrapped my arms around her when I realized she was going to be a while.

"It's okay," I whispered, patting her back lightly.

She cried brokenly into my neck, and I looked over to see Attie doing much the same to the kid. *Mace.*

He gave me a nod, and I returned it before I started for the front door,

Aspen still in my arms.

"Your brother's going to be here soon," I told her, starting to reach for the front door, which burst open before I could capture the handle with my fingers.

Downy rushed through, a look of pure panic etched across his features.

"You okay?" He questioned, pulling Aspen from my body and crushing her into his arms.

"Yes!" She wailed

The room filled up, then.

Police. Firefighters.

They filled Aspen's living room, and chaos ensued.

"Guess it's good that we got an ambulance here since this badass took care of the problem," Tai said teasingly a few minutes later.

I gave him a look.

"I'm not thinking the fucker needs a ride in the ambulance," Downy growled. "I'm thinking he's well enough to go straight to the station."

Aspen giggled and Downy's eyes warmed slightly.

His body, though, was still extremely tense.

Wary.

Waiting.

I almost smiled, knowing for a fact that if that kid got in the car with Downy, he'd likely come back a couple of broken bones worse for wear.

Something which Luke, as well as Nico, knew as well.

"I'll take him," Nico offered at the same time Luke said, "You're not taking him, Downy."

Downy snorted and said, "You can try to stop me, but it's going to happen."

Then Luke pulled rank.

"You'll keep your shit together," Luke grumbled, walking to the boy that was now sitting in a kitchen chair with his hands cuffed behind his back.

Without another word, he took the boy by the elbow, who had sense enough not to fight the big man, and walked out with him.

"Cleaners are here to get the gas cleaned up," someone said from the front door.

Booth.

I nodded at him and let Aspen go.

"Go talk to your brother," I gestured. "I have to go talk to my girl."

"Aspen!" A woman's voice called. "Where are you?"

Aspen sighed.

"My mom's here."

I wanted to smile, but didn't dare.

"Go take care of Downy and your mom."

She nodded. "Save me in a few minutes, okay?"

I winked.

"I can do that."

"Who is in charge here?" A man's voice boomed.

That must be the father.

"That's my dad," she confirmed, before she kissed me on the cheek and slipped away to circumvent her parents coming inside.

I waited until she was out of sight, then went to find my daughter.

CHAPTER 21

Where the fuck are my cookies?
-Text from Aspen to Drew

Aspen

"Where's your brother?" My mom asked thirty minutes later. "And when do I get to meet your new man?"

I pointed at Drew.

"He's talking to our neighbor," I gestured to the two men.

My mom smiled.

"He's handsome," she said. "Older, but handsome."

I nodded.

Drew was beautiful.

Even now, his hair a mess and his eyes wild, he was a handsome devil.

"Did that man next to him get hurt today, too?" My mother questioned.

I looked back at Raphael, his arm now exposed to me, and I shook my head.

"I don't know how he got hurt," I told her truthfully, and likely never would. "But I will be sure to ask in a minute."

Raphael was like a wraith, and I wasn't really sure what his role was in anything that was related to me.

He was there, though, and I found that I liked it…even if he was quiet and reserved.

"And your brother?" Mom persisted. "What's he so mad about?"

Brows furrowing, I followed my mother's gaze to find Downy barreling towards us, gathering the attention of everyone he passed, even Drew.

"I can't begin to tell you," I informed her. "He wasn't that mad when I sent him after my clothes."

He hadn't been, either.

In fact, he'd been almost…*nice.*

Which for him was incredibly impressive.

Then I got a good look of what was in Downy's hand, and my stomach dropped.

Downy, eyes wide, came out of the house, a packet of papers in his hand, and his face white as if all color had leached out that he'd been able to get back once he'd found out I was alright.

"You…your…what the fuck is going on? What does this mean?" He asked, my mom and me looked at him.

My mom looked confused.

I, on the other hand, started to freak out.

"Downy," I said, holding my hand up. "Sto…"

He turned and glared at my father.

"Get away from me," he said.

My father's eyes narrowed.

"You can't tell me that. I'm her father. I deserve…" Downy interrupted him.

"You're not her father now, are you?" He challenged.

My father's mouth thinned, and he turned accusing eyes to my mom.

My mom, who'd already been pale, became even paler.

"Attie," I whispered softly. "Why don't you go over there and check on Mace?"

Attie's eyes, which had been avidly watching both me and Downy, turned without another word as she hurried in Mace's direction.

Once she'd reached him safely, I turned back to my mom, brother, and father.

"Guys," I started. "This isn't the time, nor place, for this."

Downy shot me a furious glare.

"Shut it," he said.

I sighed and held up my hands, knowing better than to mess with my brother when he was angry.

And boy was he angry!

In fact, he wasn't just angry. Oh no, he was livid.

All of those emotions swirled together to create the mask of fuming fury on my brother's face.

My eyes narrowed at my brother, and I opened my mouth to rip him a new one when his wife came running up out of nowhere, her arms going around Downy's chest.

What was this? A fucking family reunion?

"Don't think we won't talk about this," Downy said through clenched teeth, his eyes going down to his wife's hands that were wrapped around his chest, then back up to my mother.

My mother nodded very slowly, her eyes wide and wary as she looked back to her husband.

"I think that's best," she whispered.

Something inside me loosened, and I backed away.

"I'm going to talk to Drew," I squeaked.

Not one of them acknowledged me, their eyes still locked in a strange sort of intense stare down that I was ready to move away from.

Which I did seconds later, turning and hurrying in the direction of Drew and Raphael.

The two of them were standing loosely, but the moment Drew saw me coming he opened up his arms, holding his hand out to me as he continued to speak.

"Wasn't about me at all, but about Attie," Drew was saying to Raphael. "That would've been helpful to know."

I bit my lip and looked over to where Attie and Mace were currently laughing in the back of the ambulance.

His arm was in a sling, and he had a huge black mark over the left side of his face that was quickly becoming a bruise which would be even larger and more vividly colored tomorrow for sure.

"What happened to you?" I asked Raphael.

Raphael's eyes turned to me, and his mouth smiled.

His eyes, however, didn't.

They showed pain, exhaustion and anger.

"Got on the wrong side of my boss," he said softly. "Nothing to worry about, darlin'."

I blinked.

Drew's squeeze on my shoulder told me that I really shouldn't continue to pursue the topic, so I just nodded and turned my face into Drew's chest.

"Are you off for the day?" I asked him. "Is that why you're here?"

He dropped a kiss down onto the top of my head, and shook his head.

"No. Power's out at the station, the generator's frozen solid with no hope of getting it running, and they told us we could move home base within five miles of the station, which happened to be my house. We were coming this way because we were cold. How fuckin' ironic that we walk in on that little shithead starting a fire." Drew shook his head.

"That's why I called you earlier," Raphael said, bringing my attention back to him. "Saw the kid in his yard when you left. Watched him until I was called to report in on the status on my case." Raphael shook his head. "Think he watched your place for over an hour before I had to leave. He didn't move once."

Shivers raced down my spine at remembering how cold and methodical Ellison had looked as he'd poured gas throughout the house.

"He was going to burn us all alive," I whispered, my eyes narrowing as I remembered what he'd said and done just after seeing him point that gun in my face.

My thoughts turned south, and I wondered what would've happened had I not been able to think as quickly as I had.

"I'll check in with you later," Drew's voice jolted me out of my thoughts.

I blinked quickly as Raphael nodded once and turned to head back inside his own house, but Drew didn't move until he was well out of range.

Then he hugged me, and that one act said more than enough to me. More than any words ever could.

"You mean the fucking world to me, Baby," Drew whispered gruffly. "When I arrived and saw that gun pointed at your head…" his body shook. "I seriously wanted to cry. Scream. I almost barreled through the front door, but Booth stopped me."

My eyes followed to the other firefighters.

They'd set up a grill on Drew's front lawn and had started barbequing.

Tables and chairs surrounded the grill that served two purposes—keeping them warm while cooking their food, and feeding them at the same time.

Tai and Booth were on either side of the ambulance doors, talking to the two kids that were sitting in the open doors with their feet dangling.

Attie's head was resting on Mace's shoulder as she stared at him adoringly.

"I need to tell you more," I said softly.

Drew's body tensed.

"Let's go inside," I said softly. "Just for a minute."

Five minutes later, after I'd gotten all the words out that needed to be said, I feared for that kid's life.

"What are you thinking?" I asked, taking a step forward.

His eyes closed and he squeezed them so tight that I was worried he'd hurt himself.

Was it possible for your eye to pop out with your eyelids closed?

"I'm thinking that I should've fucking killed that motherfucker while I had the chance," his eyes opened and they were practically spitting fire.

"Drew," I stepped forward to take his hand.

He shook my hand off his and started for the door, but I threw myself at his back.

He growled and spun me around to his front, then tried to set me away from him, but I clung.

"Get off!" He hissed, eyes pissed off. "I don't want to do this right now. I don't want to hurt you, or say something that I'll regret."

I shifted myself up, grabbing his face so I could look directly into his eyes.

"You can't do anything to me right now that I'll be mad about later," I promised him.

His eyes narrowed even further.

"Oh yeah?" He asked, grabbing my hair and yanking it back. "Are you sure about that?"

My heart started to beat frantically in my chest.

He'd never been that rough with me before. However, I can't say that I didn't get a little thrill out of it.

Which I told him.

"You're what?" I asked. "Going to punish me? Have at it, big boy. I can take whatever you dish out."

He tried to pull me away from him, clearly seeing the error of his ways, but I clung even tighter.

"Don't," he ordered. "Not right now. I'm barely hanging on to my control."

I laughed in his face, then dropped my legs from around his hips.

When my feet touched the ground, I immediately dropped down to my knees and started yanking at Drew's uniform pants.

He hissed and tried to step back, but I held on, following him as I worked first the belt off, then the zipper.

His hand went back into my hair and pushed me away from him, but I held on and started yanking down his underwear, baring his hard cock to my heated gaze.

"What are you?" I asked, knowing he wasn't going to let it go this time. "Chicken?"

His eyes narrowed and he stepped forward.

I either had to take his cock into my mouth, or I'd have it shoved up my nose.

Okay, well, not really. He likely would've stopped before it'd gotten that far, but I chose to open my mouth anyway.

And he didn't stop until his cock was in the back of my throat, and I was choking.

"You want me like this?" He asked. "I'll give you me like this, but you have to take all I have to give. Don't waste my time by teasing me. I don't have it in me to be nice right now, Aspen"

I sucked the head of his cock hard as I moved my hand up to cup his balls, and his eyes darkened.

I bobbed my head with the movement of his hips, and we got our rhythm going.

He'd thrust as far into the back of my throat as I could take him before he'd pull back out again.

It didn't take long before his balls drew up.

"Ahhh, God," he moaned, pulling out.

His hand immediately went to the base of his cock, his fingers an improvised cock ring that held his orgasm at bay.

"Get up. Take your pants off. Get on the bed so I can fuck you."

I scrambled out of my pants, threw them somewhere in the general direction of my clothes hamper, and dove for the bed.

He didn't laugh, but I barely contained my giggles at how funny I must have looked.

"On your back," he ordered when I started to turn over to my hands and knees.

I followed his direction and opened my legs wide.

He picked up each of my thighs, closed them, then turned them to the side to rest on the crook of one elbow.

The other hand went to his cock, which he aimed at my entrance.

Slowly, he sank inside, filling me up so fucking perfectly that I screamed into my pillow.

My legs jolted as I tried to move them, but the strength of Drew's grip on my knees had me jerking and moving with no progress.

"You're so fucking good," he breathed, his hips jerking backwards.

He filled me again without warning, making my legs jolt again.

"Jesus," I said, my insides protesting at how far he was able to get inside of me. "You're going to break me."

"I will not," he ordered. "Move your hips with me," he urged. "That's it."

I did what little I could, jerking my hips from side to side while he continued to thrust inside of me.

His eyes had gone glassy as he looked down at where we were joined, his lip between his teeth as I gripped him firmly.

He grunted, pushing in so hard that I lurched sideways, causing my whole body to roll with the movement.

"Stay still," he ordered me, slapping me lightly on the outside of my thigh before he rolled me over completely.

I went with the movement, my knees automatically going underneath me as he stayed connected the entire roll.

Without another word he started to pound inside of me. His hand grasped tightly around the length of my hair, using it to control my movements. I began to pant with the effort it took to stave the orgasm off that I could feel building.

"Fuck, yes," he growled, his hand coming down hard on the swell of my ass.

The tips of my breasts drug deliciously along the bunched up sheets underneath my body, and I started to moan into the pillow beneath my face.

I felt Drew's thumb gather some of the wetness leaking out from between the lips of my sex, then drag it up to my rear entrance.

He eased it inside, and I saw stars.

The orgasm that'd been building caught fire as it pulsed through my body causing me to practically scream into the pillow as goosebumps broke out all over my heated skin.

My pussy and ass clenched down on the dual invasions, and my eyes crossed as the most powerful release I'd ever had raced through my body.

I felt like I was flying as ecstasy poured through me.

"Jesus fucking Christ," Drew growled, pumping his hard cock into my pussy, a bit slower as my pussy clamped down on him tightly making it harder for him to push in and out.

He emptied himself inside of me in four long bursts, filling me up and stealing my breath as he twitched inside of me.

"You broke me," I moaned into my pillow.

He ran his fingertips down my spine, coming to a rest at where his thumb still filled my back entrance.

"You should've taken me there," I whispered.

He pulled his thumb free and squeezed both of my hips.

"One day I'm going to take you here with my cock," he growled. "But when that time comes, it won't be while I'm angry. I'm going to be in complete control, okay?"

I could do nothing but nod as he pulled himself from me and walked to the bathroom, his dick sticking out of his uniform pants that were still up around his hips.

"Be careful not to drip," I told him. "It'd be hell trying to explain to the guys just what that crusty white stain is."

He tossed me a look over his shoulder, and I smiled at him.

I took the time while he was in the bathroom to clean myself up, grabbing myself a clean pair of pants and underwear.

I entered when he tried to exit, and he steadied me while looking deep into my eyes.

"You okay now?" I asked him.

He shrugged.

"I've been better," he said. "But I'm not about to go up to the station and demand an investigation into his defiling of my daughter. Although I still might broach that subject with my daughter."

I shook my head.

"It was consensual," I promised. "That I know for sure. She was pissed at the world and chose the exact wrong guy to help work out some of that anger. It's something that she had complete control over."

He nodded, his jaw clenched.

"Get dressed and meet me outside," he said, then he was gone.

This time, though, I wasn't worried about him going out and killing the kid.

No, this time I was worried he'd go out and confront his daughter, which had me hurrying to get out there.

We couldn't have that, now could we?

CHAPTER 22

That moment when you hit yourself in the face when you're trying to pull your blanket up.
-Text from Aspen to Downy

Aspen

Forty minutes later, we were in the front yard enjoying barbeque with the rest of the boys.

Naomi, who'd come to the party late, was sitting next to PD with stars in her eyes.

PD was busy staring at his phone, though, as he texted back and forth with someone, leaving me with the impression that there was somebody on the other end that was a whole lot more interesting to him than the conversation and company surrounding him.

Drew pulled me down into his lap after I'd accepted a plate of food from Booth.

"Thank you," I smiled wide.

He winked at me.

"No problem," he said.

I smiled and stretched my feet out towards the metal fire pit that was in front of us.

"I didn't think we were allowed to start a fire in the city limits," I said, tossing that over my shoulder at Drew.

Drew shrugged.

"What are they going to do?" he asked, taking a large bite of his steak. "Give the fire department a ticket for starting a fire?"

I bit my lip, then picked my burger up, taking a large bite without answering.

He was right.

What the hell were they going to do? And who would be stupid enough to give the fire department a ticket?

Apparently, my ex would be.

***

Drew

My eyes narrowed as the patrol car rolled up, and I somehow just knew exactly who the dumbass was behind the wheel.

"You're shitting me right now, aren't you?" I asked him the moment he stepped out of the car.

"You're breaking the law," he gestured to the fire.

Booth stood up and stretched the muscles of his neck, then started for him.

"I suggest you leave while you still can," Tai said smoothly.

He was the closest one to the stupid fuck, therefore the most logical one to say something.

PD wasn't far behind, shaking his head and standing as well.

"Downy and Luke are on their way back here, even now," PD told him. "Now's not the best of times."

Danny's eyes narrowed on me and Aspen, who was sitting in my lap.

"Please tell me he's not really here," I whispered into the back of her head, burying my face into her hair.

Aspen was more tense than I was, her eyes locked on the stupid piece of shit while he tried to throw his weight around.

Lucky for him, and unlucky for me, Luke and Downy showed up when they did, or it was likely that the poor excuse for a man would've ended up meeting the business end of my fist.

"What are you doing here, Danny?" Luke barked the moment his foot touched the concrete.

"Sir," Danny said. "I had multiple complaints of smoke and a fire in this man's front yard."

"You knew, as well as the rest of the department, what was going on, and that I was handling it. Why, may I ask, are you here when I explicitly told you not to come?" Luke snapped.

Danny's body tightened, but he apparently saw the error of his ways seeing as he stepped back and put quite a bit of distance between the two of us.

"Sorry sir," Danny muttered, walking back to his car.

But before he could get there, Luke stopped him.

"What's this nonsense that I hear about you suing Aspen?" Luke asked him in a deceptively calm tone.

"Uhhh," Danny licked his lips nervously, not knowing what to say.

I smiled then, knowing the little fucker was about to have his ass handed to him.

Luke may not have been the most bad of all the badasses, but he was still pretty fucking scary. Especially when he wanted to be.

Like right then.

"I'm going to tell you a few things, and I'm not going to repeat them," Luke said, starting forward until Danny was only inches away from his face. "You're going to drop whatever farce you have with Drew's woman. You and your *partner* are going to drop the charges against Aspen. You're going to be split up, because the more I dig into this partnership, the less I like it so I've decided you'll be getting a male partner." He stopped, studied Danny, and then smiled. "And you're going to keep your nose clean. I know you're a good cop. I'm not sure what's started you on this path, but you're going to get your shit together and move the fuck on without terrorizing your ex."

"And you're going to return her stuff," Downy added threateningly.

Danny, eyes wide, nodded. "Okay."

"Good boy," Luke patted his cheek. "You may leave."

I squeezed Aspen's hip, trying in vain to get her to contain her laugher.

Which she barely managed.

Until Danny got in his car and started driving off.

"None of my neighbors would've called the cops," Aspen said thoughtfully.

Except, I turned to study Raphael's house.

He was standing there, a phone in his hand, as he waved at me.

At my acknowledgement, which was to laugh and raise a hand, Raphael disappeared back into the house behind the blinds as if he'd never been there to begin with.

"What?" Aspen asked curiously, following where my eyes were still pointed.

"Later," I said. "What's for dessert?"

Luke dropped down to a seat and grabbed himself a hamburger instead of a steak.

"Not a steak?" I asked him.

He shook his head.

"That'd fill me up too much, then my wife might make me feel bad for not eating the dinner that she's slaved over the stove all day to cook," Luke muttered, tucking into the burger.

My brows rose and I pulled Aspen back until she rested against my chest.

Her head came to a rest just under my chin, and I leaned my head to the side so I could press a kiss to the side of her forehead.

"What's for dinner that she has to slave over a hot stove to cook all day?" I asked curiously.

Luke sighed.

"Spaghetti...or maybe tacos. We only have about ten meals that we circulate through, and none of them require any more than thirty minutes max cook time," he explained.

Everybody laughed, including Downy, who'd yet to grab anything to eat.

Which I knew why long moments later.

"You got a minute, Drew?" Downy asked.

I nodded, helping Aspen stand.

She sat back down in my chair, and watched curiously as I walked around the side of the house with her brother but didn't make a move to follow.

"What's up?" I asked him.

Downy leaned one arm against the side of the house, then turned to regard me closely.

"I just wanted to say thank you for taking care of my sister when I...wouldn't," he started.

"Your sister did a pretty damn good job of that herself, but I would've gladly taken that credit if it were warranted. Had I not come, she would've gotten herself out on her own," I explained to him. "And from what she tells me, you taught her a little bit of self-defense, so you should be thanking yourself for having the foresight to teach her how to move like that."

Downy looked down at his hands.

"I feel like a fool," he said. "I should've tried harder to see her when we were younger…when it counted."

I laughed then.

"You stupid dumb shit," I said. "All she wants is for you to be there with her now! She doesn't hold grudges. She's nervous and scared that she might've inadvertently pissed you off by not telling you she was your full sister. Something she still doesn't know any more about than you do."

Downy frowned.

"Guess my mom owes all of us some explanations," he muttered. "Do you mind sending her over here to me? I want to talk to her before I leave. Privately."

I nodded and offered him my hand, which he took with ease.

"Thanks," he muttered, shaking it once.

Once we disengaged, I slammed my hand down once on his back and left, careful of the snow that was still piling up around us.

Why we weren't inside, I didn't know, but it was what it was.

And if everyone felt more comfortable being outside bullshitting around a fire, then I was down.

Especially with the woman of my dreams in my lap helping me keep warm.

When I reached the seat I'd previously occupied, which was now missing Aspen, my brows furrowed.

"Where's Aspen?" I asked Booth.

He pointed to where my daughter and Mace had been sitting in the back of the ambulance, which now only held Mace.

"Where'd they go?" I asked him once I reached them.

He pointed to her house.

I nodded my thanks and went inside through the carport door, finding the two of them in the kitchen looking through the cabinets.

"Can I help you find something?" I asked the two.

Aspen smiled at me over her shoulder but didn't stop looking, Attie, however, stopped and smiled.

"I told her about the stuff we bought to make s'mores last week, which you stashed over here since you were convinced I'd eat the ingredients," she explained. "And she's looking for it."

I snorted and walked into the pantry.

I kept it hidden away, because if it was out within reach, I'd eat the fuckers.

Pulling it off the top shelf, I handed it to Attie.

"Take this outside," I ordered. "The sticks are right inside the carport door right next to the dryer."

Attie smiled at me and took off, leaving me alone with Aspen.

"What was that about?" She asked once the door slammed shut.

"Your brother?" I confirmed.

She nodded.

"He wanted to thank me for 'saving' you today," I said. "And he'd like to talk to you in private."

Her eyes widened.

"Did he say why he wanted to talk?" She licked her lips nervously.

I shook my head, and she bit her lip in worry.

"Go, Baby. He's on the side of the house. And don't be too hard on him, okay?" I murmured, pulling her into the shelter of my arms.

She looked up at me, the brightness of her eyes revealing her vulnerability.

"I love you, you know that, right?" She whispered.

I leaned down, pressing my lips against hers.

"And I love you right back. You know that, right?" I teased.

She smiled, the vulnerability in her eyes vanishing.

"Be back in a few."

"I'll heat you up a marshmallow," I promised.

She grinned and disentangled herself from my arms.

"Make it two."

I followed her out, but moved towards the fire where my daughter was roasting her own marshmallow, Mace right beside her.

"You doing okay?" I asked her.

She turned a smile up at me.

"I'm better than okay," she promised. "And I'm happy."

Mace grinned, and I realized that I liked the kid—even if it took him a long time to pull his head out of his ass.

I looked over to the men that surrounded me. My brothers. My daughter. Then over to where Downy was pulling Aspen into his arms, and I couldn't help but agree.

"No, things don't get much better than this, do they?" I asked her.

"Hey!" PD barked. "You gonna hog all those marshmallows all day long or you gonna share?"

I tossed him the bag and he caught it, pulling out his own marshmallow before picking up one of the sticks from the ground where Attie must've left them.

"You're gonna share, right?" Naomi, Aspen's best friend, asked cheekily.

PD looked at her, then back to his marshmallow.

"Nope, sorry. This marshmallow is all for me."

Then he ate it, all to Naomi's surprise.

And I wondered if she knew what she was getting into with him.

PD's heart had belonged to someone else for quite a long time, and she would likely always own it.

I couldn't help but feel sorry for her as she looked at PD with those big puppy dog eyes.

But those didn't affect him either.

Arms wrapped around my chest and I moved my hand down to cup Aspen's ass.

I handed over her marshmallow and she took it with a happy smile.

"All for me?" She teased. "Thank you, you didn't have to!"

She winked, and I snorted.

Laughing, I said, "Oh, honey. You mean the world to me. I'll roast my marshmallows for you anytime."

"That sounds dirty," she teased, pressing her body up against mine.

I snorted.

"It kind of did, didn't it?"

She nodded and offered her lips to me, which I took in the next moment.

"Ewww, Dad!" Attie said. "Get a room!"

I tossed a look at my daughter that clearly said what I thought of her teasing.

"Or you could go to your room?" I suggested.

She stuck her tongue out at me, and Mace pulled her over to the back of the ambulance, out of ear range.

"You know, they're going to get married, don't you?" Aspen said soberly.

I looked over at the two, then back at the woman that I loved.

"Possibly," I shrugged. "But only after she's graduated."

"From high school or college?" PD butted into my conversation.

I looked over at the group.

Then smiled.

"Graduate school."

EPILOGUE

Who ever invented the alarm clock should be ashamed of himself.
-Drew to Aspen

Aspen

"You're shitting me," I said. "You're really going to allow me to take it off?"

Risa Fairchild, the lovely lady who'd been so helpful during all of this, smiled.

"I sure am," she said. "But only because I need it."

I snorted and picked my foot up, clunking it down onto the table enthusiastically.

Risa laughed at my exuberance, lifting my pant leg up further, then used her fancy key to unlock the ankle monitor.

It clicked slightly, and I gasped at the sudden feeling of lightness.

"Who do you need it for?" Drew asked, stopping next to his sister and bringing his arm up to hook around her neck.

He then proceeded to pull her down and mess every bit of her hair up with his opposite hand.

"Ahh!" Risa screamed. "Stop it, you big shit head!"

I laughed, my face breaking out into a large grin.

I'd always wanted Downy to be that way with me, and slowly but surely, we were getting there.

It'd been a full week since the day Ellison had tried to burn down my house. A full week since I'd moved in permanently with Drew.

A full week since my brother started trying to be the brother that I'd always wanted him to be.

Although, that'd definitely take some time to fix. My brother had gone off the handle at first, and then had come the regret everything he'd ever said or done to Jonah and me to ever make us feel like we were unwelcome.

After sitting us all down, my mother explained—without my stepfather there—that my father was infertile. She'd also told us that after a cancer scare with my biological father—who'd been dead at the time of my conception—that they'd frozen his sperm and had saved it even after his death.

When my father realized he was infertile, he'd reluctantly let my mother use my biological father's sperm, only if she promised not to tell her kids that they weren't really his.

Which led us to Downy finding out anyway.

Secrets always had a way of coming around and biting you in the ass.

Needless to say, my father wasn't very happy with the situation. Downy, however, was.

He was like a completely different person.

And I freakin' loved it.

Everything I wanted out of life was perfect.

Even on the Danny front.

Risa had approached the DA on my behalf, and had somehow made miracles happen by getting me freed from my shackle.

It'd just taken a little bit of time to process it all, which was why it'd taken Risa so long to get here and take it off.

Despite plenty of annoyed phone calls from Drew.

I'd also had all of my belongings returned to me that Danny took when he left. Including all of the money replaced in my bank account from my blog advertisements.

Now the only thing left was meeting the parents, which we were getting over and done with in one fell swoop.

Meaning his parents, my mother, his sister's family, my brother's family, and our friends were all meeting in the same place. *At the same time.*

And nobody but us knew why.

***

Two days prior

"I want to get married," I blurted out.

Drew's beer paused halfway to his lips.

"What?" He asked, turning away from the breakfast I'd cooked him and fully towards me.

"I want to get married," I said again, turning to look at Attie who was currently knocked out on the couch, then back to him.

His eyes filled with laughter.

"You do?" He teased. "Who are you going to marry?"

My lips thinned, and my eyes narrowed.

"You know exactly who I'm going to marry, Dillweed," I snapped. "And I got these nifty rings to review."

His eyes went down to the silicone rings I'd received from a new distributor that specialized in making rings for people in demanding jobs such as firefighters, mechanics, police officers and such.

His eyes went down to the ring I had in my hand, then back to me.

"Are you asking me to marry you?" He asked.

I shrugged.

"I guess. I wasn't really trying to demand *it ...but I wanted you to know my* position *on the matter...in case you were wondering," I* stammered.

He grinned and pushed the ottoman away from him before standing fully.

He left the room and came back moments later, his hand holding a pink velvet box, *causing my heart to start pounding.*

"Well, I was going to save this until we had somewhere special to go, but I guess now is as good as time as any," he said teasingly. "Do you want to switch?"

*His eyebrow was raised, and the corner of his lip was tipped up in a small quirk that mine answered with their own grin a*s *I tried not to laugh at the craziness of what we were doing right then.*

"You were going to ask me in a romantic proposal?" I whined. "I would've waited for that!"

He tossed the box into my lap and snatched the black ring with the thin, red line through the center *of it.*

"This is cool," he said, stretching it slightly before he pushed it down on his ring finger. "And it fits good. Where'd you get this?"

I told him the name of the business that'd sent it to me, and his lips tipped up.

"That was right next to the place where I got yours," he said. "Open it."

Looking down into my lap, I picked the box up, lifted the lid slightly and peaked in through the narrow opening as I immediately gasped and opened it all the way.

"How'd you know?" I gulped, pulling the ring out and sliding it onto my finger.

He shrugged.

"Thought it was cool," he said. "And I saw it pop up on the side of your computer each time you got on Facebook. It was one of the ads that showed 'you also might like this' shit. Found that one at the store and thought it looked an awful lot like that one."

It was a simple ring. And I loved it.

The band was two colors, black and white diamonds. The two alternated all the way around the ring, and I'd loved it at first sight.

I didn't know why I kept going back to looking at that ring, but now that I saw it sitting on my finger, I wanted to cry in joy.

"Thank you," I whispered, looking up at him.

"Can I call you grandma when the baby gets here?" Attie teased from her perch on the couch.

I tossed the empty box at her.

"Only if you allow me to spank you as if you were my child," I shot back.

She snorted as she stood and threw her arms around her dad's belly.

"I'm glad he picked you," she said. "I can't wait until grandma meets you."

I gasped, tuning my horror filled eyes to Drew.

"We can't get engaged yet," I said, pulling the ring off my finger and handing it back to him.

He wouldn't take it.

"No takebacks," he laughed, shaking his head and backing away

I glared at him.

"We have to make sure your parents like me first!" I assured him. "What if they hate me? Christmas will be incredibly awkward if that's the

case."

He shook his head. "Honey," he said, moving closer to me. "My mom's going to love you."

I took a deep breath.

"But what if my mom doesn't like you?" I asked.

"Your mother likes me," he said.

"They don't know you." I told him. "I can't marry someone that my mother hates."

"Wanna bet?" he asked, pulling me up snugly against his side. "All mothers like me."

I shook my head.

"You're full of it."

"You call your parents, and I'll call mine. I have a week off starting this Saturday. We'll meet up at Beaver's Bend. That's about halfway for my folks and halfway for us. Sound good?"

I nodded, but I couldn't help the nerves that took flight in my belly.

Maybe I was ready.

***

So there I was, sitting on the edge of the bed, staring at two dresses. One was a simple black number that hit me right above the shins. The other was a white number that flowed all the way to the bottom of my ankles.

"What should I wear?" I asked Drew, looking up to find him doing push-ups next to the window.

He looked over at me, then moved his eyes to the dresses without stopping.

"Black. You'll get the white dirty," he puffed out.

He then moved to the jumping push-ups, his hands alternating close and wide. In. Out. In. Out. His hands moved as if he weren't even trying.

If I were to be doing the same thing, he'd likely have to pick me up off the carpet.

"I feel like I'm going to barf," I said, counting for him in my head.

Ten. Fifteen. Twenty-three. Thirty-five.

On and on he went until he reached a hundred.

Then he stopped, went up on his knees, and stared at me.

Sweat trickled down his neck and arms in rivulets, and I had to clamp my teeth shut to keep myself from licking my lips.

He'd already ran a full two miles while I barely walked one, and then he'd started this as soon as we'd gotten back to the cabin we were renting.

Attie was staying with his parents, in the cabin next to ours, although they weren't there yet. All of our cabins were in a row, so we didn't have to go far to find the rest of our families.

We'd been the first to arrive, and I kept tossing surreptitious glances out the window to see if I could get my first glance, even though I knew they weren't going to be there for at least another hour or two. I wasn't sure if they were unloading their car first, though, so I kept peeking.

We were actually meeting them at a restaurant that was fairly popular for the crowd gathering in Beaver's Bend.

"What has you so nervous?" Drew asked. "You need me to do anything to take your mind off it?"

He leaned forward and started stretching his calves, planting both fists into the carpet and leaning back on one foot.

The muscles of his arms bulged, and I swallowed, the familiar tingle in my pussy flaring to life as I watched the sexy man move.

"Uhhh," I said smartly.

He switched arms and moaned as the stretch worked its magic on the sore muscles of his legs.

"Aspen?" Drew grinned, panting lightly. "What are you doing?"

I stood up and stripped my clothes from my body, revealing the garter belt, hose, and matching panty and bra set I'd slipped on after my shower.

He hadn't seen it before, and I'd been saving it for tonight. However, the way the sweat was clinging to his body, as well as the way his eyes seemed heated, made me forget my good intentions.

The road to hell is paved in them.

His head came up when I dropped the t-shirt that was covering my upper half, his eyes dragging along my legs and stopping when he found out exactly what I was wearing…up close and personal.

"What are you doing?" He repeated, his voice having dropped at least an octave in about thirty seconds flat.

"I'm using you," I told him, walking up to him until my pussy was just a few inches from his face.

His hands came up to rest on my hips, and I smiled.

I had him.

"You think the maid comes while we're out?" I asked him.

He nodded.

"That's what the chick at the front desk said. They come twice a day, and most of them try to come during the evening hours while the folks are out for dinner," he said, licking his lips, then leaning forward to place a kiss right above my panty line.

I stepped back out of his reach, then challenged him with my eyes.

"I want the maid to know I was well fucked in this room when she comes to check on it later," I whispered, backing up until my knees hit the bed with a soft thump.

Drew smiled, taking his shirt off by hooking his hand in the collar at the back of his neck and bending over to pull it swiftly from his body.

"I'll see what I can do," he said, standing up to start on his shorts.

I bit my lip, causing his eyes to zero in on the move.

He always got so hot when he saw me do that. I didn't really know why, but I found myself doing it way more than I needed to just for the simple fact that I liked his reactions to it.

I sat down heavily, then rolled over to present my ass to him.

He moved up behind me; his hairy thighs met the backs of mine.

Then his cock probed my entrance and I smiled.

"Don't rip my panties," I told him, looking over my shoulder at him.

He must not have heard me, because the next thing to go were my panties, and not in a nice way.

I gasped and shoved up on my elbows to look at him.

"Drew!" I said in surprise. "I just paid fifty dollars for this bra and panty set!"

His eyes caught mine and darkened.

"Don't care," he muttered, sliding the length of his cock down the lips of my sex and back up again.

I moaned into my pillow, turning my head so I could bite the edge of one.

These were small cabins, and there wasn't much room between our cabin and my mom's cabin. The same went for the ones his daughter was currently in. So, I tried to be as quiet as I could be.

I didn't want to make this day any more awkward than it was already going to be by allowing them to hear my sounds of ecstasy scarcely an hour before this first meeting.

But then Drew thrust his fat cock into me, and I realized that that was a stupid idea anyway.

I had no control when it came to Drew.

If he wanted me to scream, which, obviously, he wanted me doing right then, then I'd fucking scream.

"Give me your eyes," he ordered, pulling my hair.

I screeched.

"Don't touch my hair!" I ordered him. "It took me nearly thirty minutes to get these curls perfect."

He ignored me, pulling my hair until I was back up on my hands and looking at him over my shoulder.

Then he started to pull out of me before filling me back up again. Long, strong thrusts that had me panting in a matter of moments.

His eyes stayed locked with mine while he did, and I very nearly lost the battle before it'd even started.

His abs contracted and relaxed with each thrust, and his eyes went down to where we were connected, breaking the contact that was holding me hostage.

My head went down to the pillow, but he obviously didn't want that because he pulled my hair back again.

I had two choices; either look up so he'd loosen the hold he had on my hair or endure the pain.

Obviously, I wasn't averse to the pain, but I chose to look at him since I knew that was what he wanted.

He licked his lips when I moved my eyes back to his, and then he slowly moved his finger to my back entrance after coating it with my secretions.

My eyes widened, as they did every time he did this, and he smiled.

"Yes?" He asked.

I bit my lip and nodded.

This would be the time he went all the way. I knew that almost instantly.

We'd been working up to this for a while, and I was ready.

He worked his thumb around my back entrance, teasing me remorselessly until finally he pushed inside.

My mouth dropped open in surprise at his abruptness.

It didn't hurt, per se, but it definitely took some getting used to.

It was then I realized somewhere in between my contemplation he'd found some lube.

Where, I didn't know, but I was quite thankful for it, too.

Especially when one finger turned into two, and then two became three.

Soon I was pushing back on three fingers, and moaning so loud that I probably sounded like I was dying from an outsider's prospective.

Added on top that, his cock continued to thrust inside of me. I was turning into a needy mess.

"Please," I whispered, pleading for something—*anything*—with my eyes.

He grinned then and pulled out of my pussy, and I watched in awe as he tipped up the lube bottle that he'd magically produced and poured a generous amount onto the palm of his hand.

I blinked.

"Don't get that all over my body," I whispered gutturally. "I've already taken my shower."

He grinned.

"Oh, honey, when I'm done with you, you're going to need another shower."

Then he was there, his cock at my back entrance, and pushing inside.

It didn't go at first, and my eyes started to water.

"Oh, God," I whispered, unable to control what was coming out of my mouth.

His teeth gritted.

"Relax," he whispered gruffly. "Push out."

I did, and then I swear I saw stars, and not in a good way.

"Jesus Christ," I whispered, my knees going out from under me until I was flat on my belly in the bed.

My asshole felt like it was on fire as he followed me down.

Once he got the head of his cock inside, the rest followed easily, and I was left panting when his hips met the cheeks of my ass.

"I'm dying," I moaned as the burn continued.

His hand snaked around between my hips and the bed, easily finding my clit with his still lubed fingers.

And then he did some more magic, making me relax in small increments while he stayed as still as he could.

It took a few long minutes of me panting, as well as him circling my clit, before I finally relaxed enough to start feeling something other than pain.

"I think," I panted, turning my head back to the side. "That all of our play could've never prepared me for you."

He grinned and leaned forward, placing a kiss to my neck.

The move pushed his cock further into me, and this time, instead of pain, I felt pleasure.

It was an odd pleasure, but pleasure nonetheless.

"Ohh," I breathed, my eyes going wide.

He went up to his elbows on either side of my head then, and slowly started to move in and out of me.

Softly, *lovingly*.

"There you go," he breathed into my ear. "Relax and take me."

I did, my eyes closing as I let the movement of his hips carry me away.

"I…" I hesitated. "I think I want to be on top."

Maybe if I had more control over the entire thing I'd be able to enjoy it a hell of a lot more.

And I did.

The moment he rolled us to our backs and I automatically pulled my feet up to lay flat on the bed.

The roll had us coming up slightly sideways, causing one of his legs to be sandwiched in between mine.

Sitting up, I used his upraised thigh to get me there, and immediately moaned when his thigh met my throbbing clit.

"Jesus," I breathed.

His hands went to my ass as he started to push me up and down on his cock.

"I feel so full," I whispered, crying out each time he dropped my hips.

He pushed and let me fall, and we followed that pattern for quite a few thrusts when things started to change.

And he could feel it, too.

No longer did it hurt.

No, it just felt beautiful and perfect.

I held onto his knee as he started to move me even faster, up and down I went on his cock, holding on as he did all the work for me, and crying out each time my ass met the cradle of his hips.

"Oh, God, I'm there," I whispered roughly, my head falling back.

My clit started to pulsate, and then my pussy convulsed as my orgasm swept over me.

I held my breath instead of screaming, heart beating wildly, as my release overwhelmed me.

Drew's hands on my hips started to pull me down even harder and rougher, and what started out as beautiful turned into magnificent as I had my first out of body experience.

Drew's belly tightened as his release took him over, soft grunts punctuating each time his come spurted from his cock, bathing my insides in his essence.

"I think," I panted long minutes later. "That we're going to be late."

Drew laughed.

"I don't know what gave you that idea," he muttered, pulling me down to his chest and kissing the side of my neck.

I turned until my lips met his.

"It was the clock on the wall," I informed him.

He laughed and we scrambled out of bed, and I was thankful that the housekeeping would be visiting while we were away. If they were to come in while I was still there I might very well combust in flames of embarrassment.

***

Downy and my mother kept giving me weird looks all night, but my soon-to-be mother-in-law and father-in-law absolutely adored me.

Something I was absolutely certain of two hours later.

"You know who this is, don't you?" my mother asked me.

I blinked, turning to face my mother and Downy fully.

"Who? What are you talking about?" I asked in confusion.

"You remember that summer we came to Beavers Bend? The time when mom forced me to go, and I stayed with that kid the entire time?" Downy asked.

I did remember. It'd been terrible.

My mother and father had done nothing but fight for hours about how Downy didn't spend any time with the 'family.'

And I'd been the one to take the brunt of that.

Meaning my father forced me to stay away from them in an attempt to get away from the fighting.

I'd spent the entire time outside, watching.

I watched as Downy and that 'kid', as he liked to call him, had a grand ol' time, and I didn't.

"Yeah," I said slowly. "Why?"

Downy grinned.

"I didn't put two and two together until I saw his parents," he pointed at

Jacklyn and Ryan. "They haven't aged as much as him," he pointed at Drew. "I specifically remember you telling me that you would marry him one day."

That's when my mouth opened.

I had said that, but I hadn't put two and two together until Downy had just pointed it out.

"You married that woman, and I told you it wasn't a good idea!" I pointed out to Drew.

Drew then laughed his ass off, as well as his parents, as understanding dawned.

I'd told him the same thing the day he'd told his parents that he was marrying his ex-wife.

"We brought up that comment for years," Jacklyn said as she wiped her eyes free of the tears that'd formed during her laughter.

I grinned.

"I aim to entertain," I informed them.

Drew pulled me into the curve of his arm.

"You definitely please me, baby," he whispered into my hair.

I looked up at him, at his smile and the light shining in his eyes, and squeezed him tight.

Attie looked over at me, and she winked before mouthing, "Told you."

I stuck my tongue out at her, and then enjoyed the rest of my night in the arms of the man that I knew since the age of nine that I'd one day marry.

I was happy indeed.

***
Seven months later

"Does it look bad?" I asked my brother.

My brother studied my face, and, fucking straight as could be, he said, "It looks fine."

I took him at his word, too.

That was until Drew lifted my veil twenty minutes later, and his eyes zeroed in on the hideous thing.

"It's bad, isn't it," I said softly.

He shrugged. "I said for better or for worse, didn't I?"

My mouth dropped open, and then I started laughing. Right in the middle of my wedding, with my hundred and twenty of our closest friends and family in attendance.

"Dad," Attie whispered in affront to her father. "You're not supposed to tell her that her pimple looks bad. She'll take it the wrong way."

Drew's smile widened.

"Well, I also promised to tell the truth. Which vow would you rather I follow?" He asked with a raise of his eyebrow.

I grinned.

"Both," I said. "You follow both."

He winked and pulled me into his chest, placing a kiss on my nose.

My growing belly—something we only learned about last month—pressed into his taut one.

"Freakin' crazy girl," he said. "I don't care about your pimple. Your face isn't why I'm marrying you, anyhow."

I smiled.

"Why do you want to marry me?" I questioned him.

He grinned.

"You really want to know?"

"I do," I said.

"I love you because you make me feel happy. Because you make me sleep well at night. Because you make me laugh. Because, when I wake up beside you, you make my heart race. Things like that."

Those were almost the exact words I'd spouted off to him twenty years ago.

"You just got bonus points," I informed him.

He grinned and winked, knowing exactly what he'd just done…*and earned*.

I patted him on the hand, meaning he should let me go.

He did and I turned back to the preacher.

His eyes hit on the pimple, and I narrowed my eyes.

"Ignore it!" I barked.

The preacher grinned and resumed the ceremony, and soon I forgot all about anything but Drew.

That was until Attie's water broke thirty minutes into our reception.

An hour later, we were holding Attie's daughter, Sienna Drew, in our arms.

"Dad!" Attie said loudly. "Give her back."

Drew looked at his daughter, and then back down to his granddaughter.

"Why?" He asked. "You got to have her for nine months. It's my turn!"

I snorted and took a seat, my wedding dress poofing up at the sides.

The door to the room burst open and Mace, in full army fatigues, burst through the room.

"I didn't make it!" He fake wailed.

I rolled my eyes as Mace walked up to Drew and fell in love with the little girl at first sight.

"Oh, boy," I said to Attie.

Attie smiled at me, and I smiled back at the love I could see shining in her eyes.

"You did good, baby girl," I told her softly.

"With the man or the baby?" She whispered back.

I looked back at the three of them, then back at her.

"Both. You did good with both."

Attie smiled and then bellowed.

"Can I have my baby now?"

Drew glowered at her.

"I already said no!"

I chose to laugh instead of strangle him.

I had priorities, after all.

My main one being I wanted to use the man on my wedding night, not bury him.

***

Downy

3 months later

"Downy." My wife said through clenched teeth. "It's time to grow a pair."

My eyes narrowed. "Memphis, I do have a pair. How do you think you got two kids out of me, and another one on the way?"

Memphis grinned.

"Just do it." She ordered yet again.

Sighing, I walked to the door of my house, and opened it for my sister.

She stared at me like I'd grown a second head.

"What's wrong with your face?" She asked.

I rubbed my cheek where my beard had to be shaved due to some stitches I'd received about an hour ago.

"Punk thought it'd be funny to sucker punch me in the face while I was ordering a sandwich at Subway." I murmured.

She looked at my cheek, up to my eyes, and then back to my cheek.

"Maybe he was offended by what you put on your sandwich." She offered.

I narrowed my eyes.

"There's nothing wrong with adding ketchup to my fuckin' sandwich!" I yelled.

Memphis started to snicker from somewhere behind me.

"Did you ask me over here to yell at me, or did you have something more to say?" She asked, crossing her arms over her chest.

I looked over my shoulder to see my two kids playing in the middle of the living room, then gestured her to come inside.

"Follow me to the den." I said. "I have something to show you."

She followed behind me, and I closed the door once we got inside, gesturing to my desk with a tilt of my head.

She looked at me suspiciously.

"What?" She hesitated.

I pointed to the desk, and she finally let her eyes trail away from mine.

"What is this?" She asked.

"That," I smiled, proud of what I'd done. "Is the apology that I should've given you a long time ago."

Words escaped her as examined it, and then a large smile overtook her face.

"This is a picture of Danny getting arrested."

"I pressed charges on him...and his woman."

She blinked. "What?"

"Being the assistant chief of police has its benefits." I told her. "And when I found out that Danny had ten unpaid tickets—ones that his partner had tried to have buried—I got him. It wasn't much. He'll never see jail time...and likely won't lose his job since we're so fuckin' low on officers...but it made me happy."

She picked up the picture frame, the one holding the photo of Danny in cuffs being herded into a police car with my hand on the top of his head guiding him down, and beamed.

"I'm going to hang it up by my bed." She declared.

"I'm sure Drew's gonna love that." I snorted. "Let me know how he likes it."

She turned those eyes—the ones exactly like mine—to me and stared.

Then she gently placed the frame down onto my desk, and promptly threw herself into my arms.

"I love you, Downy." She whispered. "It scares the shit out of me each day you put on that badge, but I'm so freakin' proud of you."

My arms tightened around her.

"I love you, too, Aspen."

She squeezed me just a little bit tighter before letting me go.

"But I'm still not admitting that ketchup is an acceptable sandwich topping."

I ruffled her hair, knocking her ponytail sideways. "Well, somebody has to be wrong in this life. It might as well be you."

She gave me a look that clearly said she didn't agree.

"What's for dinner?" She asked, changing the subject.

"Eggs."

"Let me guess. Scrambled eggs and ketchup."

"If you don't like it, you know where the door is." I informed her, knowing she wouldn't leave.

Her smile was brilliant.

"I'm not staying for the eggs. I'm staying for the good company."

We walked out of the den arm in arm, and I was glad I had my arm around her when Lock slammed into her the moment we'd crossed the threshold to the living room.

"Aunt Pen!" He screamed. "We're getting another puppy."

My mouth dropped open.

"Who the hell told you that?" I snapped.

"Mommy said."

"Mommy most certainly didn't say that!" I told him. "I said she was having another baby, not a fuck…"

"Downy, you finish that curse word in front of my kids, and I'll forget you like your socks to match for the next week."

I snapped my mouth shut and glared at my wife.

"You wouldn't."

"Try me." She countered.

Aspen started to snicker. "I can't wait to see what three babies do to your gray hairs."

I sighed.

"Fuckin' a."

"You got that right, big brother."

A flourish at the door had both of my kids screaming in excitement as their Uncle Drew came through the door, and I grinned when both latched onto his legs.

"You did good with him. You know that, right?" I asked my sister.

Aspen's eyes met mine.

"I do." She promised.

With my arm wrapped around her shoulders, we both watched her man as he allowed my kids to take him down on the ground and start crawling all over him.

Aspen pulled away when it looked like the kids were getting to him, and then joined the fray, sitting directly on Drew's back and tickling him from behind.

"I like this." My wife said from beside me.

I looked at my wife and agreed with a nod of my head. "I do, too."

ABOUT THE AUTHOR

Lani Lynn Vale is married to the love of her life that she met in high school. She fell in love with him because he was wearing baseball pants. Ten years later they have three perfectly crazy children and a cat named Demon who likes to wake her up at ungodly times in the night. They live in the greatest state in the world, Texas. She writes contemporary and romantic suspense, and has a love for all things romance. You can find Lani in front of her computer writing away in her fictional characters' world...that is until her husband and kids demand sustenance in the form of food and drink.